DESTINI

DESTINI

Johnny Bullard
White Springs, Fla.

Cover photo courtesy of Joyce Marie Taylor

Edited by Joyce Marie Taylor

Printed in the United States of America

Dedication

This book is dedicated in loving memory of my beloved uncle, the late Gary Edward Bullard, November 18, 1931- April 15, 2017. Thank you for always loving me unconditionally, for always supporting me, and for always believing in me. I shall always love you.

I also dedicate this book to my editor, Joyce Marie Taylor, Live Oak. Without your hard work, candor and belief in me, there would be no books by Johnny Bullard. Thank you, Joyce. God bless you.

Finally, to the wonderful people "Around the Banks of the Suwannee" who provide inspiration for me, I thank you.

As always,

From the Eight Mile Still on the Woodpecker Route north of White Springs, wishing you a day filled with joy, peace, and above all, lots of love and laughter.

Johnny Bullard

"We are but as the instrument of Heaven.
Our work is not design, but destiny."

Owen Meredith (1831-1891)

Chapter 1

"Oh, lordie, it's goin' be a sizzler today!" Destini howled, as she hopped into her bright red pickup truck and cranked the engine. "Let's get this show on the road!" she added, and then she steered the truck toward the main drag that would lead her out of the small community of Seraph Springs.

It was just past the noon hour and she was on her way to Turpricone at the north end of the county. The air conditioner was on full blast, but it seemed to be taking longer than usual for the cab to cool down, as the intense heat of the mid-day sun was pouring in through the untinted windows.

"Cool me down, baby!" she shouted, as she aimed all the A/C vents toward her face. "I shoulda paid the extra money to tint these darn windows," she grumbled. "Good ol' hindsight. It'll get you every time."

Even with the windows rolled up and the air conditioner cranked to its limits, Destini could still smell the earthy, pungent odor coming in through the vents from the side-by-side chicken farms off to the right side of the highway. About a quarter mile up ahead there were two more chicken farms that had recently been built by the same owners. On the opposite side of the street there were several pig farms that stunk even worse than the chicken farms.

"Smelly, smelly town," Destini mumbled. "I guess you just get used to it after you've lived here for a while… or not!" she added, laughing.

As she approached Old River Road, she had an epiphany and decided to act on it. There had been lots of talk recently about a new business that had come to Seraph Springs and it was all kind of hush-hush in the beginning. It still was, quite frankly, but it didn't stop the rumors from swirling around all over the county.

It seemed that thousands of acres of land just north of the old farm where Destini's grandmother Mama Tee was born and raised, and still lived, had been purchased by some foreign investment group. Destini's brother and sister-in-law, Duke and Essie Wilson, also lived not far from there.

It was rumored that this investment group had paid premium prices for all the acreage they bought, which was less than half a mile from the historic Suwannee River.

Destini hadn't had an opportunity to check it out yet, because she had been so busy handling things at Camp EZ, as well as caring for her young daughter, and trying to keep up with her friends' lives, among many other things.

"I have a few extra minutes today," Destini declared. "Maybe I'll see for myself what's going on."

With that, she made an abrupt right turn off the main highway and onto Old River Road. About ten minutes later, she pulled off to the side of the road, put the truck in Park, and let the engine idle. She sat there for quite a while just taking in the sights and recalling things she'd been told about what was going on.

Right in front of her, about a hundred yards ahead, was a gigantic iron and steel archway over top of two very wide electronic gates that evidently lead into the secret farmland property, which was fenced in with barbed wire. In big, bold letters above the archway was the name *Feed the World Organics*. Above the name was a large and impressive looking globe that was also fashioned out of iron and steel.

Destini had heard there were six entrances along Old River Road surrounding the entire property, but the main entrance was the one that really stood out.

"Dang," she muttered. "All them rumors was right about this place. I got me a bad feelin' about this, though," she added, as she eyeballed the place. "Yes sir-ree, I do. Somethin' just don't feel right."

B.J. Gorman, a longtime resident of Seraph Springs, a trusted welder, and an old friend of Destini's from high school, had told folks that the archway and all the gates had cost *Feed the World Organics* close to two-hundred-thousand dollars.

B.J. was an educated, hard-working, Christian man and also an artist in his own right in later years. He had sold several of his sculptures to prominent individuals throughout the region, as well as to a few museums across the country, so when he spoke about anything, people tended to believe him.

He was quoted as saying that these new farms were "growing various produce crops, such as carrots, turnips, collards, kale, soybeans, corn, and numerous varieties of squash." That all sounded impressive at first glance, but folks in the county soon began to worry that it was going to turn into a vegetable crop monopoly and put all the little guys out of business.

The local water authority and other governmental entities involved with water-use permitting... in the words of Louise Frayburn, who was a friend of B.J.'s and employed by the water authority... said the permits had been "issued like Chiclets to a sugar-hungry child."

The company, B.J. told her, was registered in the state of Florida, but the primary officers in the corporation had rather nondescript names, like Sara Smith and John Jones.

"Yeah, right," Destini thought, as she recalled all the things B.J. had told her about the place. "I wonder who the real owners are."

News reports from several major campaigns across the state of Florida had stated that *Feed the World Organics* had made hefty contributions to a number of political campaigns recently and in past years, including some on the local level in Campbell County, which didn't surprise Destini in the least.

What was surprising, however, was that the company was issued a special permit by the local water authority that allowed them to self-monitor their own water usage. When Destini heard that part, she knew for certain there had to be something sinister going on, or at least something illegal.

Additionally, B.J. said there were three huge warehouses deep within the property and far away from prying eyes. Inside those warehouses, he said, equipment and supplies for the farms were kept, although, there were many skeptics who had their own ideas as to what was really hidden within those walls.

Not long after *Feed the World Organics* took ownership of the land, an entire village of hundreds of brand new mobile homes, as well as a few modest cinder block homes, was built on a portion of land at the northwestern end of the property. There were so many migrant laborers working the land that the federal government even offered to build them a pre-school, utilizing a grant that was secured by *Feed the World Organics*. Those grant funds were distributed so quickly that it made people's heads spin, too.

The company even had their own health clinic, built in record time, by the way, which really ticked off the local residents, who had been trying to find funding for a clinic for Seraph Springs for years, all to no avail, so far.

Then, all it took was one visit from an official of the organization to the health department in Campbell County to meet with the director to determine that *Feed the World Organics* would be better off hiring their own medical director to oversee the clinic. Supposedly, it would be licensed under the auspices of the proper authorities in Tallahassee. It was all very shady, Destini thought when she heard about it.

"Too damn shady," she mumbled.

The health department was permitted only at certain times that were determined by *Feed the World Organics* to come in for routine inspections. Most of their inspections, however, were submitted electronically to an office in Tallahassee, so in reality, there was little, if any, local involvement or oversight.

The company claimed in a newspaper article a few months back that all their crops were utilized to feed the poor in Campbell County, as well as in developing nations, and that everything was grown organically. They assured anyone who would ask that no chemical pesticides or insecticides were used on the crops. To date, Destini hadn't heard of anyone locally who had benefited from their farms.

"Because it's all a lie, that's why," she mumbled.

She recalled part of the sub-headline in a newspaper article she read: "No commercial fertilizers are used in growing our crops," said Dimitri Smith, one of the foreign investors of *Feed the World Organics*.

At least two dozen center-pivot irrigation systems had been placed on the property, B.J. had told her. Reportedly, several dozen deep wells had been permitted to pump countless gallons of water needed to grow the crops. Nearby neighbors, including Mama Tee, Duke and Essie, said they could hear the irrigation guns, as they referred to them, pumping all day and all night.

One thing that was truly odd about the entire situation was that nobody local was allowed on the property without proper notice.

"Pretty creepy, if you ask me," Destini said, as she watched a big diesel-fueled pickup truck approach the gate. "Mind your own business," she muttered, when she saw the driver staring at her, as if she was about to commit a criminal offense or something.

Feed the World Organics was like a city set unto itself covering some fifteen-thousand acres of farmland and former timberland that had been cut and stripped clean of all its timber. From Old River Road at certain vantage points, if you looked hard enough, you could see the workers' village and the corporate offices.

There were lines and lines of pine trees and oaks, as well as indigenous shrubs blocking the view of most of the activity going on behind all those gates. Destini was told by B.J. that a lot of the old shrubs and trees had been purposely left alone across a good portion of the farm near the highway, in order to "add ambience and to respect the local flora and fauna." That was according to the owners, of course, but in reality, it was to veil the back fields where the real farming operation was taking place.

"About all I can see right now are all those streams of water being shot into the sky way back in there somewhere," Destini said, as she squinted out the passenger side window. "Well, I'd best be gettin' on with my business or I won't make it back to Camp EZ in time to fix supper."

࿇ ࿇ ࿇ ࿇ ࿇ ࿇ ࿇ ࿇ ࿇

DESTINI'S MISSION today, and her reason for the trip into Turpricone, was to purchase locally grown vegetables at the farmer's market co-op. It was the closest farmer's market to Seraph Springs and their prices were more than competitive. She would be serving the fresh produce to the guests at Camp EZ, her place of employment for close to two decades now. She would also buy a little extra for her family and friends, as she had been doing for years.

About thirty minutes into her journey, she rolled into downtown Turpricone, the county seat of Campbell County, which sat about fifty miles from the Georgia border in north central Florida. A familiar sight caught her eye, as it always did when she ventured into town. It was a huge digital clock sitting atop the old bank.

The time showed it was ten-twenty-seven, if you cared to believe it, that is. Whether it was a.m. or p.m. really didn't matter. The weathered old clock was perched like a beacon on top of the now-shuttered Continental Planters Bank. It blinked the same exact time twenty-four hours a day, seven days a week. The flashing temperature on the reverse side of the clock registered a steady sixty-eight degrees, even though it was the middle of September and hotter than a four-peckered billy goat right now. Again, just like the time readout, the temperature never changed twenty-four hours a day, seven days a week.

Each time she saw the clock, she felt as if she was being hurled into a time warp, as if she was a bit player in an episode of the *Twilight Zone*... or at least the town of Turpricone seemed to be stuck in a time warp, she thought.

Old as the clock was, however, it still managed to spin around on its axis the way it had for the past fifty years, only now it was whirring around on a rusted metal pole and getting rustier by the day. The intermittent screechy sounds would grate on your nerves if you were near it for very long.

At one time, the bank building was a beautiful showpiece for the community, but now it only looked lonely and derelict, a lot like many of the current residents of Turpricone, Destini thought with a chuckle.

Just seeing the old, broken clock as she drove through town, caused her thoughts to reel back in time to a different era. She recalled Campbell County's phosphate mining company, Consolidated Regional Applied Phosphate. They had employed thousands of people from Turpricone and nearby Seraph Springs over the years. The company was so big, in fact, that they hired many dozens of folks from outside the county, as well.

With so much tax revenue pouring into the county's coffers and so many people looking for a place to eat lunch, a place to buy groceries and clothing, and all the other life essentials, the downtown shops and restaurants were thriving.

The days of the huge phosphate boom, however, were long gone. Currently, they employed a couple hundred people as they continued their business, albeit on a much smaller scale.

The mining operation had accounted for the bulk of the county's tax revenue ever since they came into town over sixty years ago, but as they kept downsizing in more recent years, those funds were dwindling to the point of becoming an emergency situation for the future of Campbell County.

It was a struggle for the town leaders to bring in new business, as there wasn't much incentive for a company to locate there or, more importantly, for people to live in such a poverty-stricken county, which is exactly what it had turned into.

As a result of the continuing lost revenue from the phosphate company, as well as the departure of many of Campbell County's citizens, who had gone elsewhere to live and work, the area schools and businesses were in a steady, deep decline, and there seemed to be no hope for a better future. The only new ventures of late were some farms that had sprouted up around the county, but they, too, were struggling in the weak economy.

The county not only looked tired, but it looked completely defeated; the downtown area, especially. It was desolate and many of the buildings were in total disrepair. Turpricone seemed only to be a pass-through for all the interstate truckers who were heading north or south to the larger cities to pick up and deliver goods. All those heavy semi's were tearing up the roads like there was no tomorrow, too. It was actually quite sad because Turpricone was such a bustling town in its heyday.

One of the last businesses to close was Miss Sissy Paquette's beauty salon, Betty's Beauty Box, which Destini just came up on. Why Miss Sissy never changed the name of the business after she bought it was still a mystery, as she refused to divulge her reason for keeping the old name, no matter how many times she was asked.

Today, all the windows were boarded up and graffiti in a variety of faded colors was smeared all over the entire building. The old sign out front had been vandalized numerous times and now it only said "ty's ty ox".

Destini spotted a couple of guys leaning up against the side wall, who, from the looks of them, were most likely homeless. They were sharing what looked to be a cigarette, although, one never knew these days what people were smoking, she thought.

"What a shame," Destini said, shaking her head, as she drove past the building. "What a darn shame."

Not long before Miss Sissy had left town, she had quipped to Destini, "Got to move on darlin'. I can't make it on a few sets and comb-outs for old ladies… old ladies like me, you know," she had added with a chuckle. "I need a little something more."

"I hear ya, sister," Destini had replied.

"My great-aunt passed away in New Orleans and left me a pretty little two-story house that has a garage apartment," Miss Sissy had told her. "I think I'll rent that out and maybe go back to work for one of my old boss men, Etienne Colour."

When she was in her early twenties, Miss Sissy said she went through a rebellious stage and moved to New Orleans from Jackson, Mississippi, where she was born and raised. That was when she first met Etienne Colour. She said she was out scouring the entire city hunting for a job to keep her off welfare when she came upon his small shop off the beaten path. He hired her on the spot, she said, as one of his longtime stylists had died suddenly in a car crash the previous day.

"He has a shop not far from the French Quarter called Coiffures by Etienne," Miss Sissy had told Destini. "He always said I could do the fastest finger waves of anyone he ever saw. Call me, honey, I remember him saying. Come for a visit to the Big Easy, he said. You know what, Destini? I think that's exactly what I'm going to do."

Just reminiscing about all the good times she and her friends shared with Miss Sissy, got Destini to thinking. She reached into her pocketbook for her cell phone. It was old, but it still worked, and she had just refilled it with more minutes using a card she bought at the Daily Dollar yesterday. She pulled off to the side of the road and punched in Miss Sissy's number in New Orleans. She answered on the second ring.

"Coy-fures by E-tee-ahnn, Miss Sissy speakin'."

"Well, Miss Sissy, guess who?" Destini asked, without even trying to disguise herself.

"Destini Wilson! Oh, honey, it's so good to hear

your voice! Are you calling me from your gold-plated Cadillac, baby?"

"No, ma'am, I ain't," Destini said, laughing. "I'm still drivin' this pickup I bought not too long ago. How are you, Miss Sissy?"

"Better, now that I'm talking to you, and loving it here in New Orleans! When are you coming for a visit? How are our friends, Nadine and Wanda Faye?"

"The girls are busier than one-armed paperhangers. Between their mama, their husbands, the children and the Women's Center, they are some kinda busy."

"Don't I know it, sweetheart? I would love to see y'all," Miss Sissy said.

Destini could hear the chewing gum popping in her ear and could picture Miss Sissy in her mind, as if she was sitting right in front of her. Her bleached blonde hair would be teased high up on her head, and she'd be smiling wide, showing off her big pearly whites and her ruby red lipstick.

"Well, are you serious about me visiting, Miss Sissy?" Destini asked. "I would love to come see you. I'll bring Dee Dee with me, too, assuming she can get her doggie nanny to take care of Chanel for a few days. You know she won't leave that dog in a kennel."

"Oh, my," Miss Sissy said, laughing. "She has a nanny for her dog? That big ol' Standard poodle?"

"Are you kidding?" Destini asked, laughing herself now. "She thinks that dog is her child. I ain't never seen a dog get so much pamperin', but that's Dee Dee for ya. She's got a big ol' heart and evidently a big soft spot in that heart for four-legged creatures."

"Well, God bless her," Miss Sissy said.

"Anyway, we're gettin' into the busiest time of year at Camp EZ, but Wanda Faye and Nadine, I'm certain, would agree to manage the camp while I come for a visit," Destini continued.

"All right, then!" Miss Sissy shouted. "And, yes, of course, I'm serious about you comin' for a visit! Honey, you've just made this old girl's day! Oh, to heck with that. You just made my next few weeks, sweetheart! Come on down! The gumbo is already simmerin' in the pot and the Big Easy is waitin' for that hurricane from the flat woods of north Florida, Hurricane Destini!"

"Thank you, Miss Sissy," Destini said. "God bless you. I haven't had any time to myself since Mr. Hamp's passing. I really need some time away."

Hamp Brayerford had been an institution in Seraph Springs, as well as in the entire county. He was a banker, a landowner of thousands of acres of timberland, the founder of Camp EZ, a gracious humanitarian, and most importantly to Destini, he was the father of her young daughter, Easter Bunnye.

"Of course, you need time away, honey. We all need time to ourselves once in a while," Miss Sissy told her. "You come on over here any time, honey. We'll cut up worse than gorillas in Sunday school. Then, we'll paint the town hot pink, bright red and orange. Maybe all three at the same time!"

"Thank you, Miss Sissy. I'm looking forward to our visit. Don't know if I'll fly or drive, but I'll phone you when I make up my mind. Some of it depends on Dee Dee's schedule. It might even be closer to Christmas."

"Whenever, honey. Plane, train or motorcar, the welcome mat is out and the party will begin when you get here," Miss Sissy squealed. "I'll even take some time off work so I can hang out with you girls."

"Okay, then. Sounds good. See you soon, Miss Sissy," Destini said, smiling wide with anticipation, as she listened to the familiar sound of hairspray being applied to someone's head in the background.

"Bye, hon, can't wait!" Miss Sissy shouted, and then she hung up the phone with a loud clunk.

Chapter 2

The next month-and-a-half went by in a flash and before Destini realized it, she was sitting in the back seat of a chauffeur-driven limousine and headed over to Jacksonville International Airport. Her cousin, Carl Alvin Campbell, had made all the travel arrangements. Her final destination? New Orleans, Louisiana.

As soon as she arrived at the airport, she was escorted to the VIP lounge. Moments later, she heard the clicking of heels against the hard tile floors of the airport terminal.

"I know that walk," she said.

There was no mistaking it. When she turned around, there in a killer black ensemble, accessorized with heavy silver jewelry, of course, was a fashionable vision of beauty; her cousin, Dee Dee Wilson.

"Destini!" Dee Dee shouted, as she ripped off her designer sunglasses. "Honey, we're not here for a long time, we're here for a good time. The party is here!"

"Girl, you crazy!" Destini gushed, and then she greeted her cousin with a giant-sized hug.

"What's our flight number?" Destini asked.

"Baby, we don't have a flight number," Dee Dee coyly replied.

"Huh? We driving? You bring your car?" Destini asked.

"No, honey, we are not driving. We are flying. You see that Gulfstream jet over there?" she asked, pointing toward the large window behind Destini. "That's the one we're going on. It's a private jet and we have our own special little pilot. I think his name is Captain Weaver or something like that. Anyway, we'll have the entire airplane all to ourselves, baby. It's a direct flight right into New Orleans. Oh, and snacks from Camp EZ will be ready for us as soon as we board the plane."

"You kiddin' me, Dee Dee?"

"No, ma'am, I am not kidding you. Now, while they're getting the plane ready, let's go over to the bar and have a Mimosa. Our plane will be ready in about a half hour. Let's relax, laugh, and talk for a little while, and then we'll be ready to go."

"Sounds good. By the way, how's your man?" Destini asked, as the two women sat down on a couple of lush, leather barstools.

"Honey, he is just as fine as he can be… and sweet as honey, too, baby."

"Ain't love grand?" Destini quipped, rolling her eyes.

"It sure is," Dee Dee concurred. "You should give it a try sometime."

"I'll pass on that for now," Destini said.

"Oh, bartender! Two Mimosas, please!" Dee Dee shouted at the old man behind the bar, who was serving drinks to an elderly couple about ten stools down. The old couple looked as if they had just returned from a funeral, judging from their black attire.

The bartender looked over at Dee Dee and nodded that he understood her order.

"Anyway, Ricardo's a good lookin' man and you goin' have to keep an eye on him," Destini said. "He's the kind of merchandise that other people wanna pick up, and more than that, people wanna take home."

"They can want as much as they want, honey, as long as they don't take the merchandise out on approval. There'll be none of that goin' on, sweetheart," Dee Dee said. "I know all about those kinds of shoppers. I've been in retail for a long, long time."

Both of them had a good laugh, and for the next half hour they talked and reminisced. Destini told Dee Dee how much she appreciated her making the trip with her and how much she looked forward to seeing Miss Sissy. Before they realized it, it was time to board the airplane.

As the young ladies approached the plane, Destini spotted a short, small-statured steward, who had his back turned to them. There was something about the way he stood that she recognized.

Suddenly, Destini yelled, "Mark!"

Mark Evers, Miss Sissy's former assistant at Betty's Beauty Box, turned around. When he saw who it was, his face lit up and he smiled at them, showing off his perfect, white teeth.

"Coffee, tea, or me, ladies?" he asked with

outstretched arms.

"Mark! What in the world?!" Destini gushed, totally flabbergasted to see an old friend hanging out at the airport.

After they all hugged each other, Mark told them, "I have a part-time job with this company and these private planes working as a flight attendant. I didn't know until yesterday that it was you two who were going to be on this flight. When I found out, I got so excited I almost peed myself. I must warn you, though," he added. "I haven't had a lot of sleep."

Seconds later, he escorted the two of them down the ramp and onto the spacious and luxurious private jet and told them they could take a seat anywhere they wished.

"Magazines? A glass of champagne? Anything?" he asked the two women.

"I'll take a glass of champagne," Dee Dee said, as she got comfortable in one of the oversized lounge chairs toward the rear of the plane.

"Nothin' for me," Destini said. "Thanks for asking, though."

Instead, she sat down, or rather, she sank down into a comfortable, plush seat across from Dee Dee, closed her eyes and promptly fell asleep within seconds, due to total mental, emotional and physical exhaustion. She never knew when Mark put her seat belt on, when he took it off, or when he put a blanket over her during the flight.

Destini Wilson, heiress to a fabulous fortune in

Campbell County, thanks to the late Mr. Hamp, had drifted off into dreamland. She found herself going back in time to when she was working as a part-time domestic, maid and nanny in some of Campbell County's most prominent homes. In the first part of her dream, she saw herself, hair freshly straightened, a white uniform, white shoes, and she could hear a child crying in the distance. She knew the cry, so she reached across the dreamlike fog to little Watson Jarrellson Williams and she held him in her arms. Watson was the first child she cared for as a nanny. She was fourteen-years-old at the time.

In another scene, Watson was three years old. She could see his beautiful, willowy mother, Anna Mary Jarrellson Williams. Then, she saw the boy's tall, angular-faced, severe looking daddy, Stanley Williams. Stanley was an engineer with the state's largest utility company. In fact, he was the chief engineer. He was a Georgia Tech graduate and a native of Massachusetts.

Destini recalled the story her grandmother, Mama Tee, told her about Anna Mary's marriage to Stanley. She had explained how the Jarrellson family – the last of the area's old cotton aristocracy, or as close to it as Campbell County could muster – threw some kind of fit when she announced she was going to marry Stanley. It was just after her sophomore year at an exclusive women's college in Virginia. Anna Mary, it seemed, didn't really care what her parents thought about the matter. She was determined to marry Stanley, no matter what.

For over three decades, the entire Jarrellson clan had been supported by Anna Mary's father's eccentric brother, Spencer Augustus Jarrellson, or Uncle Gus, as he was known to Anna Mary. Uncle Gus made his fortune through investments on the New York Stock Exchange, primarily by purchasing blue chip stocks from several well known utility companies. It was through Uncle Gus that Stanley Williams obtained his position at the utility company.

Anna Mary, always the apple of Uncle Gus's eye, never lacked for anything. If Stanley Williams couldn't provide for her, Uncle Gus, very diplomatically, of course, always took up the slack.

The old Jarrellson home, which was situated on a high bluff in Seraph Springs close to the Suwannee River, had been completely renovated and redecorated before Anna Mary's marriage to Stanley.

After emerging from a three month honeymoon across Europe and the United Kingdom, Anna Mary walked into her new family home, which was decorated to look as if it had gone back in time to when Sea Island cotton had been King.

Uncle Gus, in addition to being a savvy investor, was also a visual artist of some renown. His watercolor paintings of the flora and fauna of the upper Suwannee Basin fetched incredible prices at galleries all over the world. One of his paintings even hung in the White House in Washington, D.C., in the president's Oval Office, no less.

Despite his fame, however, Uncle Gus didn't travel

a great deal. He actually preferred the solitude of his small cottage with its spacious studio where he could paint to his heart's content. The cottage sat like a small watchtower in the night, smack dab in the middle of a hundred acres of luscious, wooded forest. It was so peaceful and serene that he often said he felt he was living in another universe. It was only a small portion of the thousands of acres once owned by the Jarrellsons before the War Between the States.

Thinking of the baby again, Destini dreamed about the times she sat with Watson in the old, wooden rocking chair that used to creak in the still of all those silent nights. She always sang him to sleep with the words of one particular song.

"All night, all day, angels watching over me, my Lord.
All night, all day, angels watching over me."

For many years, Destini actually did serve as Watson's angel in her own special way. She had tried many times, without success, unfortunately, to alert Anna Mary about what she felt was Uncle Gus's less than natural attention to young Watson. Anna Mary was oblivious to the facts, though, and never addressed the situation.

As Watson grew older, he began accompanying Uncle Gus when he went to his studio and with increased frequency, which Destini thought was disturbing, to say the least. Anna Mary, however, had a full social schedule to occupy her time and she merely seemed relieved to get the child off her hands for those periods of time.

Stanley, on the other hand, was a working machine and he paid no more attention to young Watson than to a new piece of furniture or a new set of dishes. To him, the child was just a "thing", like a new television or a new sofa. When he left home in the mornings the "thing" was asleep, and when he came home late in the evening the "thing" was asleep again. Unlike the British upper class, or even his wife, for that matter, he never attempted to spend just an hour a day with the child.

There were some rare... extremely rare occasions that Stanley did spend with his son when he was about two years old, such as holiday photos that his wife insisted upon, brief outings in the pool when he was caught off guard, or short walks in the garden when he was actually trying to sneak off to have a cigar. Of course, Destini was never far behind, as it was her job to keep an eye on the child. Stanley became adept at saying to Watson in a somewhat soothing manner, "Here's Destini," which always made Watson giggle, but made Destini feel awkwardly out of place.

Meanwhile, because of Stanley's absence in the boy's life, Uncle Gus became the child's world and he soon took over young Watson's life, as if he was his parent or his own personal guardian angel. He seemed to always have time for the boy and Watson would jump up and down with delight anytime he saw Uncle Gus. In fact, the first word the child learned to say was Gus, which pleased the old man to no end.

Destini, though, felt in her bones that something wasn't quite right between the old man and the little boy. With her suspicions at the center of her heart, she decided to see for herself what was going on between them. Unfortunately, it took some time because she was so busy with her chores that she had barely enough time to breathe, let alone spy on the old man.

Five years flew by in a hurry. Destini, along with Anna Mary later on, was most concerned because Watson was now in second grade and he still had frequent occurrences of wetting his pants. He experienced regular bouts of enuresis, as Anna Mary referred to her son's bedwetting. Each night, it seemed, the white cotton sheets got soiled. As time went by, the boy's mattresses experienced a short shelf life, to say the least.

Destini knew enough about the matter from hearing Mama Tee and old Doc Campbell's daughter, Miss Aggie, talk about children who experienced periods of withdrawal that led to bedwetting. According to them, the children were extremely shy and were often the victims of unwanted attention from either a relative or friend, which would cause the bedwetting. Miss Aggie went a step further, and in a whispered tone, she explained that it was "unnatural" attention.

It was the last part of the whispered conversation that eventually forced Destini to evaluate young Watson's situation and do something about it. She was determined to find out if anything was amiss. Despite

Mama Tee's warnings about staying out of white folks' business, Destini made her way down the lane leading to Gus's cottage one afternoon.

She peered through the picture window at the rear of the cottage and what she saw next was more than shocking. She had suspected it for some time, but now, seeing it up close and in person made her shudder. She put her hand to her mouth, as tears barreled down her cheeks.

"Poor little baby," she thought. "Sacrificed on the altar of money and molested by his own great uncle."

Nobody would believe her, she figured, as she pondered what to do next. In reality, she knew they *wouldn't* believe her. They would elect *not* to believe. It was easier that way for all concerned, she thought, but she felt she had to do something and quick.

She sprinted all the way to Mama Tee's house and was out of breath when she finally made it to the front porch. Mama Tee was sitting there in her special chair, slowly rocking back and forth, as if she hadn't a care in the world, when she suddenly stopped. Mama Tee seemed to have a sixth sense when trouble was approaching and today was no different.

"You breathing hard girl," she said, turning her head toward Destini. "Tell me what wrong wid you," the old woman demanded.

"Mama Tee, Mama Tee, Mr. Gus is messin' with that baby! I saw it myself! I don't know what to do!"

Calmly, as if she had nerves of steel, the unbreakable Mama Tee said, "What you do is pray, chil'. It's all you can do."

"But, Mama T..." Destini started to protest, but her grandmother stopped her.

"You tell the sheriff, you think he ain't goin' go and tell them white folks? You put yourself in danger, girl. Them folks has taken old man Gus's money for years. That chil' is ruined already. All you can do is pray that he ain't too messed up. This is one of dem situations you ain't got no bidness messin' with."

"But, it's wrong, Mama Tee!" Destini shouted. "It's wrong!"

"The only chance with that chil' gettin' any help, be for you to tell Hamp Brayerford, honey. You go tell him. He might go to dat chil's daddy and do some good. Even dat be risky, though."

Mama Tee's head swayed back and forth behind big, dark glasses. Her sightless eyes, though, saw much more than most seeing folks. A moment later, she spat a stream of tobacco juice in a tin can that was beside her rocker, as Destini stood in front of her praying for an answer to the dilemma she was facing.

"My a'vice is, you leaves the white folks' bidness alone, girl," Mama Tee began. "They cause you a heap o' grief widout any dem paying you no mind 'cept firin' you. You know what that means, girl? No job nowhere in dis place for you 'cept dat nasty chicken processin' plant."

Destini sat on the edge of the porch, still breathing hard and with fresh tears streaming down her face. "I gots to do it," she told herself. "Hell may break loose, but if it saves what's left of dat baby…"

With that, she walked the five miles over to Hamp Brayerford's cabin on the Suwannee River, which the Jarrellsons referred to as "that new timber trash". She sat in the shadows until well after dark, not even taking a drink from his outdoor faucet until she saw the headlights from his old pickup truck coming down the winding lane.

As she was wiping her mouth with the back of her hand, he called out to her even before getting out of his truck. Mr. Hamp always seemed to instinctively know when something was wrong, just like her grandmother.

"Destini?! Your Mama?! Mama Tee?!" he shouted, as his face showed signs of genuine concern.

"No, suh," she meekly replied. "More dan dat."

So, she told her story. Mr. Hamp never doubted her, either.

The following day, she received a note inside her monthly pay envelope, which was all in cash, as was typical. It was a lovely note written by Anna Mary.

Dear Destini,

Words cannot express the thanks Stanley and I have in our hearts for all you mean to our family, including Watson. Your influence upon his life is without measure. More than anything, we appreciate your continued prayers and hopes for "our" baby.

We have decided that Watson needs a more structured environment than can be provided in the educational setting of Campbell County. The little school in Seraph Springs has served its purpose, but I am going to send Watson to live with his paternal grandparents up in Massachusetts where he will have a more fitting educational setting. In a few years, he will attend the same boarding school where Stanley attended.

Uncle Gus has gone to Italy for an indefinite stay to paint and to drink in the culture, as if he needs to go there. He practically lived there for a decade. Watson will only be coming home now at Christmas. We will certainly contact you when he visits here, as he will want to see you.

Again, with all our hearts, Stanley and I thank you.
Ever,
Anna Mary

There was no "sincerely", no "yours truly", and not even a "your friend" in the closing... just the word "Ever". Destini gave her credit for that, at least. She found out much later that Mr. Hamp had visited Uncle Gus and told him he would kill him, or worse, expose him to all of North Florida, if he didn't leave town immediately. He also read the riot act to Stanley and Anna Mary, and threatened to call the local child services organization if they didn't do as he asked.

Soon after that, Anna Mary joined the Women's Missionary Society at the local Methodist church for the first time in her life and she became quite active in their programs. Stanley started attending Sunday morning worship services, too. Then, for the first time in the decade the two had been married, they knelt together at the altar rail to partake of communion.

When Destini heard about it, she went to see Mama Tee.

"It ain't the blood of Jesus they drinking," Destini told her. "It's the blood of that baby on their hands and they know it."

Mama Tee merely smiled and nodded in agreement.

Meanwhile, Uncle Gus never did make it to Italy. On the second night out at sea, one of the stewards heard a loud boom coming from his stateroom. There was no mess. Uncle Gus had taken the plastic liner of the shower curtain, wrapped it around his head, and pulled the trigger. In his coat pocket they found his last will and testament. It was dated three days before he left New York City for his trip to Italy; the trip he never completed.

About a month later, his assets were doled out as follows: A trust generating two-hundred thousand per year for his niece, Anna Mary Jarrellson Williams, to be used by her in any way she saw fit. The remainder of his assets, totaling approximately fifteen million was left entirely to his great-nephew, Watson Jarrellson Williams. It was to be administered by Uncle Gus's personal legal representative, Elwood Ellison Carter, Esquire, Attorney at Law in Jacksonville, Florida. There was a special proviso attached to the will that stated Watson's parents were never to touch those assets, nor have any access to them... period. Additionally, any and all expenses incurred against the estate would be regularly monitored and checked by Mr. Carter or a member of his law firm.

Chapter 3

In her ongoing dream during the flight to New Orleans, Destini watched the years fly by. She saw young Watson as a teenager during his rare visits to Seraph Springs. His parents never knew, but each year on her birthday, at Christmas, and at Easter, the boy would see to it that Destini received a crisp hundred dollar bill. The bank in Turpricone always had an employee phone Destini. It had been the same employee for over a decade. After each call, Destini would go to her office to receive her gift.

After Watson entered medical college in Massachusetts, Destini heard of his brilliance in the area of psychiatry, which became his specialty. She also heard of his struggles with who and what he was, which didn't surprise her after all he had been through as a child. She later heard through the grapevine that he was in love with one of his fellow medical school classmates; a young girl from China, which pleased her to no end.

Watson went to China with her to visit her family and that was when he fell in love with the Far East. The two of them carried on a long distance relationship for a short while. Unfortunately, on one of her trips back to China, she was killed in a car crash and he was completely devastated.

After he graduated and completed his residency, he wound up going back to China because he simply loved it there. Then, he traveled extensively throughout Asia and eventually took a job as part of a cultural exchange program at a hospital in Peking.

Watson's parents never visited while he was in China. Anna Mary would simply tell her friends around the bridge table that her baby was doing well and that he just loved it there. She said she and Stanley were planning to visit him next year, next year, next year... but they never did.

After a short time working at the hospital, things took an unexpected turn for the worst for Watson, and in a huge way. Destini blamed it on his early upbringing and the abuse he suffered at the hands of his Uncle Gus, which caused him to become confused about his gender identity.

His troubles began when the hospital board in Peking decided it was time for a changing of the guard, so to speak. They'd had the same administrator at the hospital for the last twenty years, and they felt it was time for some new blood and some fresh ideas. So, they interviewed and eventually hired a new administrator, who happened not to be pro-Western or pro-American.

Just days after the new administrator took over the reins, Watson found himself terminated. In fact, he wasn't only terminated, but he was later asked to leave the country, as he was in a great deal of trouble, which wound up causing a major international diplomatic snafu in the end.

From what Destini had learned, Watson had befriended a young Chinese boy, who was part of his English tutorial class. It wasn't long before the two became more than teacher and student, and more than just friends. The young man's mother, a high ranking government official, came home one afternoon and witnessed something happening between Dr. Watson Williams and her son.

She immediately reported it to the government. Watson was arrested, thrown in jail, and was subjected to an almost immediate trial with no proper legal counsel. After a conviction was levied upon Watson, a government official stated that his sentencing would be a public execution, since it involved a westerner who, in their opinion, violated the trust of a gullible sixteen-year-old Chinese boy. They insisted the execution was justified and it was to be carried out within the next two weeks.

Word of Watson's dilemma made it back to Seraph Springs a few days before the scheduled execution. It was only after several million dollars had been expended by the Williams' family out of Watson's trust fund, that the sentence of public execution was downgraded to a public caning. Watson was beaten within an inch of his life with a thick wooden rod, and the entire scene was televised all over China.

After the beating, Watson was marched through the streets where people spat on him, threw trash at him, and cursed him for being a dog. Watson had said that walk through town from the place of his torture was pure hell.

After hearing about Watson's crime, the hospital administrator insisted on his immediate dismissal, and the government put him on a plane to the States with nothing but the clothes on his back. Everything else he owned was confiscated by the government.

Watson later learned that the administrator was a second cousin of the girl with whom he was deeply in love, and he blamed Watson for her death. He was told she was hurrying to catch a plane in the corrupt West, when, in a moment of unfocused attention, she was hit by an automobile within a few steps of the airport terminal. She happened to be clutching a recent photo of Watson in her hand, and it was rumored that his name was the last word she ever uttered.

Watson found himself "a man without a country" with a disgraceful medical career behind him that he might never rectify, on top of his broken heart. When he got back to the States, he turned to alcohol and drank himself senseless night after night. Eventually, he became so distressed that he voluntarily checked himself into the Ocean Breeze Rehabilitation Center in Panama City Beach in the Florida Panhandle.

At that time, the azaleas had just begun to bloom and the Gulf coast was magically clothing itself in new green flora and beautiful, pastel-colored flowers, as it prepared for the Easter season. It was there that Watson met Monty Wu.

Monty's mother, he learned, had named him after Montgomery Clift, her favorite movie star of all time. He was the result of what old folks in the Deep South would refer to as a misalliance. It seems his mother was a southern siren trying to make it in the movies, but she had to go back to Mobile, Alabama to give birth to her son. He turned out to be tall and thin like his beautiful auburn-haired mother, but with the features of his Chinese father, who worked at the movie studio as a security guard.

Monty had no conscience when it came to bettering himself with O.P.M.; Other People's Money. He heard of Watson's travails in the Far East while in confidential counseling sessions and he made himself available to talk, confide, or listen whenever he ran into Watson.

Using a filched master key to the fireproof filing cabinet inside the safe, and with the access code to the master file on the computer, Monty found out all he needed to know about Watson. One interesting thing he discovered was that the shoes Watson usually wore weren't the simple slippers that were issued to all the other patients at Ocean Breeze. That little tidbit may have seemed minor to some, but to Monty it was just what he needed to formulate his master plan and it worked like a charm.

It didn't take long for Watson to become intrigued with Monty's idea for a psychiatric hospital, located in a remote area of the Deep South. It was property that was perfect for such a place, according to Monty, and it was right on the Gulf coast of Florida.

When he described the place, Monty smiled and said, "Warm southern breezes, moss-festooned trees, mockingbirds singing, and azaleas in bloom, like a vivid portrait of Southern beauty."

Watson instantly fell for the idea and suggested he serve as the medical director of the hospital, while Monty could serve as the overall administrator.

"This place will rival any of the best psychiatric hospitals in the nation," Watson told him.

"I agree," Monty concurred. "Plus, it will only be available to select clientele."

"Absolutely!" Watson shouted in agreement.

All went well with the plan, until the medical director at Ocean Breeze phoned Mr. Elwood Ellison Carter, Esquire, who handled Watson's finances. Mr. Carter phoned Watson's parents and after a rather lengthy luncheon meeting in his private office, Mr. Carter embarked on a little trip to Ocean Breeze Rehab Center and asked to speak to Watson.

Watson was clearly surprised to see the seersucker-suited Mr. Carter appear at his door, but he was pleased to see him, nonetheless. He was even more surprised when Mr. Carter asked to speak not only with him, but with Monty Wu and Dr. Samuel Geiger, the medical director. Mr. Carter told Watson before the meeting that he had been assured by Dr. Geiger that he was near the point of being discharged from the hospital and that he was medically well enough to hear some straight talk regarding Monty, as well as learn about an interesting clause in his Uncle Gus's will that dealt with his finances. Once they all gathered together in a small conference room, and after preliminary greetings, Mr. Carter began his discourse.

"Watson," he started, stone-faced and serious. "Your financial life has been a lot of my life for over twenty years and it pains me to have to tell you this, but it seems your Uncle Gus had placed a small proviso in his will regarding you. I now have the sad duty to read you part of that stipulation. You've never asked about it, and I've never had reason to bring it up to you, but the truth is, unless you marry and produce an heir, your money cuts off in about eighteen months. Your trust dries up and it goes to your mama and daddy and the Seraph Springs United Methodist Church."

Watson was shocked and it showed on his face, as he glared at his longtime attorney in disbelief.

"Let me see the papers," he demanded, and Mr. Carter handed them over.

What Watson didn't know was that the papers had all been recently typed up with a typewriter Mr. Carter had kept in good repair over the years. Knowing the proclivities of the rich, Mr. Carter guarded his clients and his own well-being with the cunning of an old wizened fox that had eluded more than one hound.

After reviewing the documents, Watson spoke.

"Wha... what does... what does this mean?" he stammered.

"What it means, young man, is that you have a wonderful medical education and you've had a privileged life. You can live off what you make as a doctor, which, if you're enterprising enough should be substantial, but you won't receive a dime from the trust set up by your Uncle Gus, unless you fulfill the parameters of what is set forth there. It's all pretty straightforward. Currently, your trust, as a result of careful investment, makes about twenty-five thousand a month, which is at your disposal. You have traveled, been educated, gone to the finest schools, by the way, and had all the advantages your uncle's money could provide. Even through uncertain financial markets, I have safeguarded your trust and kept a steady stream of income for you, but beyond that, my hands are tied. Either you marry and produce a legitimate heir within eighteen months, or, to be blunt, it's bye-bye to millions for you."

Watson was still in shock and he clearly had no idea how to respond to this unbelievable news, so he just sat there looking dumbfounded.

"And, now, if y'all will excuse me, I will leave these papers with you, so you can read it over some more. For now, though, I must move along. My sister, Sophie, and her family are patiently awaiting my arrival in Mobile. I hear there's a big pot of seafood gumbo waiting on me with my name on it, along with some of Sophie's scrumptious crab cakes. Call me, Watson, when you have time to think things over, son, and good luck. You have my prayers for your full and complete recovery. Thank you Dr.... uhh, young man," he added, nodding in Monty's direction, and he left the room.

It took less than seventy-two hours for Monty to have his resignation requested by the hospital's administrator, and he immediately departed with a month's severance pay to parts unknown.

Dr. Geiger and the other members of the hospital board felt the money was well spent on Monty's compensation packet, and they hoped they would never see him again.

Within two weeks, young Watson Williams was on his way home to Seraph Springs.

"Home," he said, as he rounded the curve in his brand new SUV. "I haven't called this place home in close to twenty-five years. I sure do miss all those happy days with Destini when I was a kid."

A smile spread across his face, which was quickly replaced with a frown when, on the home's enormous front veranda, he spotted his parents. His mother was standing just outside the front door dressed in a flimsy, pastel-colored dress, and with her hair in the same old style. He called it the rich lady's cut. It was a chin length page-boy, and, as always, she was wearing the ubiquitous headband with the small, colored ribbon on the side.

His father, on the other hand, had always reminded him a bit of England's Prince Philip from what he had read in textbooks; aloof and disinterested in anything that was not part of his world.

As Watson alighted from his car, his mother came down the steps with her arms outstretched, as if they were the perfect, loving family greeting one another after a long absence.

"It's so good to see you, Watson," his mother said, and she clasped him in an embrace that was more for show than anything else, although, who she was trying to impress was anyone's guess.

Watson's arms, however, stayed limply at his sides without returning the pretentious hug, although, he did manage to utter, "Good to see you, too, Mama."

When his father extended his arm, Watson shook his hand.

"Hello, Father," he curtly said. "Slim and trim as always."

"Well, you know, son, it must be all that swimming, biking and walking... a lot of walking, by the way... plus, I never eat meat," his father bragged.

"Yes, of course," Watson said. "Well, I guess you won't be joining me for dinner then, because I plan on going straight into town to the Smoking Pig Barbecue. I've been hankering for those mouthwatering ribs for months now. Mama, would you care to join me? I'm not going for another hour or two."

"Why, yes, sugar, I would love to join you," she said. "Yes, that sounds perfect. Your father will come, too, won't you, Stanley? You can have the onion rings and the big salad. We'll make a family outing of it."

As Watson was heading up the stairs to settle in and unpack his bags, he was mumbling to himself.

"Yep, we're just a big loving family," he joked. "A big, phony, loving family."

Chapter 4

The Smoking Pig that evening was jam packed, as always. Merilee, one of the waitresses who had worked there since as far back as Watson could remember, waltzed over to their table with a huge smile plastered on her face.

"Well, well, the whole Williams family," she said. "Young Mr. Watson. Ain't this nice? Haven't seen you in a month of Sundays. Mr. Williams, Mrs. Williams, what'll it be?" she asked, as she stood poised to jot down their dinner orders.

Watson ordered a large plate of barbecued pork ribs with all the fixin's to go along with it. Anna Mary opted for a barbecued fish sandwich and Stanley ordered the big salad with a side of fried onion rings, just as his wife had suggested earlier. As soon as Merilee dashed off to the kitchen, Anna Mary reached across the table and took hold of Watson's hand.

"Honey, I know you have experienced a rough patch, some choppy waters, you know, but that has run under the bridge, as it were," she told him. "There will be no judgments from your daddy and me, Watson. I want you to rest, visit, take long walks, and when you're ready, I'd like to throw you a small party… but not until you're ready, darling."

Watson seemed totally disinterested in what his mother was saying, as he took a sip of the sweet iced tea that one of the other waitresses just placed in front of him.

Rather than outright ignore his mother, though, he half-heartedly responded, "Sure thing, Mama. Whatever you want." Then, out of the clear blue, he added, "I'd like to drive out and see Mama Tee and Destini."

"Well, of course, sugar," she said, with her signature fake smile plastered on her face. "I believe I still have Destini's cell phone number somewhere. You'll want to phone her first and see when she's not working at the poultry plant, though. I'm sure her hours and shifts vary, just like everyone else who works there."

Watson's face turned a bright shade of red, and it was clear he was outraged at what he just heard coming from his mother's lips. He managed to keep his calm, although, it took him a few seconds to stop the anger that was welling up inside of him from spewing out like an erupting volcano.

"One more thing, Mama," he began, without raising his voice, but looking her straight in the eyes. "Destini is to be offered a job back at the house immediately. I don't care what she'll be doing, but I want her to have her job back. She never told anything but the truth about what happened to me, and she was punished for it. That punishment ends now," he sternly said. "I will attend your party and meet whatever local, simpering fools you have lined up for me to meet, but

Destini comes back to work. If she doesn't come back to work, Mama, believe me when I tell you this... I may not have the trust money behind me, but there will be enough that I will make certain... absolutely certain, that this part of the world is fully aware of why Destini was let go at the house and what she knew."

Both his mother and his father sat with their mouths agape, stunned by Watson's declarations. Meanwhile, Merilee returned with their food and placed it all down on the table. She obviously sensed something was wrong, so she quickly turned and left. Within seconds, Stanley shot back at his son.

"Destini Wilson will *not* come back to work at my home!" he barked through clenched teeth, trying to be as quiet as he could without the other restaurant patrons hearing him.

"Your home?!" Watson haughtily responded, not caring who around him was listening, and they were. "Your home, Father?!" he kept on. "You'd better go to the property appraiser's office there, Pop. It never has been *your* home. It was always in Mama's name, as well as all the other property owned by the royal Jarrellson family. None of it is in your name. Not a piece of furniture, and not even a sterling teaspoon engraved with a "J". The day you said "I do" and took Uncle Gus's money to go to Europe and then into the historic Jarrellson house, they bought and paid for you just like they bought over a hundred slaves before the War Between the States."

"Watson!" his mother gasped. "I am shocked that

you would make such a crass statement!"

"Oh, Mama, please..." Watson said, brushing her off with a backhanded look. "Come, now. Let's eat our barbecue and talk about the weather, or this year's camellia show you hosted... something, anything," he said, as he picked up his fork. "We can even talk about Uncle Gus's paintings and what will be hung in the local gallery named in his honor, but let's not talk about lies. I am finished with them. I'm going to see Destini and Mama Tee after we leave here and after I drop you two off. By the first of next week, Destini will be working at the house. Now, eat up... end of story!" he declared, and then he filled his mouth with a large, scrumptious pork rib that was dripping with the Smoking Pig's mouthwatering house barbecue sauce.

Chapter 5

Aboard the private jet, Dee Dee had been reading an article about the latest trends in men's clothing in an obscure fashion magazine called "GG for Men". She happened to glance over at Destini, and saw she was acting really strange with jerky body movements, especially her hands. She was also talking in her sleep.

"Oh, goodness, did she just say Watson?" Dee Dee mumbled, as she strained to hear what she was saying.

Destini was indeed in a very deep sleep and she soon mumbled something else.

"Not end of story," she said, clear as a bell this time.

Dee Dee just shook her head and reached over to adjust the blanket over top of her cousin, pulling it up so that it covered her bare arms, as it was quite chilly inside the cabin of the jet.

Meanwhile, Destini was being drawn deeper and deeper into her dreams. This time, she saw Watson as he entered Mama Tee's small front room that late spring evening many years ago. She heard the grief and the joy in his voice, as he called out her name and Mama Tee's name, and then embraced both of them. She heard him tell her that she was coming back to the Jarrellson house to work, and would be making double what she was earning at the poultry processing plant. She saw and she heard all those things again, as if time was repeating itself.

Then, she saw the weeks flash by that she spent in the Jarrellson mansion receiving the silent treatment from both Miss Anna Mary and Mr. Stanley. She did her best to ignore their coolness toward her, as she methodically went about her work, mopping floors, polishing furniture, and preparing breakfast for Watson each morning. She spent a lot of time preparing for a big party being given in Watson's "honuh", as Miss Anna Mary would say in her thick Southern accent. This was not an ordinary cocktail party, however. This was a major, major event.

Destini overheard the calls made to caterers in Jacksonville and Valdosta. She saw the sterling silver candelabras, the silver epergnes, the complete sets of sterling silver julep cups and other family heirlooms that were brought over in an armored van from Planters Continental Bank.

Then, she visualized the day of the event, which began early in the morning on the Saturday of Memorial Day weekend. She saw tables covered with white linen, she smelled fragrant roses in big, ornate arrangements, she saw iced petit fours, cakes, cookies and sandwiches, and a bar that stretched the length of the huge solarium. She saw ladies and gentlemen all dressed in their finery, and she took it all in.

Somehow, through the music, the fragrance of the flowers, and the aroma of the food that seemed to replenish itself on the tables in wave after wave, she felt that everything that was going on that mild May evening was in preparation for something. It wasn't long before she discovered what that something was.

At about nine-thirty that evening, the party was in full swing. Couples were out on the dance floor under a huge white tent that was set up on the lawn overlooking the river. It was just a few yards away from the back porch of the mansion. Waiters were hurrying back and forth, covertly, but graciously receiving tips from men on the sly to rush their drink orders.

The twenty-piece orchestra broke into the strains of "Old Folks at Home", as a young woman, quite other-worldly in beauty, descended the stairs into the great room inside the Williams' mansion. She was dressed in a white lace cocktail dress; a sheath that hugged her body. It was tailored and perfectly fitted, but not suggestive in the least. She wore a long strand of white pearls and at her ears were sparkling diamond solitaire earrings. Her dark brown, almost black hair was styled and caught at the back of her neck in an evening chignon, and she carried a tiny, embroidered envelope evening bag. She had quite the exotic look about her, almost Asian in appearance.

The woman had the most sparkling blue eyes Destini had ever seen, and her skin was so flawless that it looked like a fine silk fabric. Although she had a tan, it wasn't a dark, dark tan. It was, perhaps, like one who spent a lot of time playing tennis or golf, she thought. She was, quite frankly, a stunning young woman in every sense of the word. In fact, Destini thought she was the most beautiful woman she had ever beheld, except for Dee Dee, who happened to be standing at the bottom of the staircase with her uncle, Hamp Brayerford, and her aunt, Hattie Campbell Wilson.

"Well, I Swanee!" Aunt Hattie gasped when she saw the young woman, using a phrase that she and her niece had made up many years ago.

"I Swanee what?" Dee Dee asked, playing along with her.

"Damn," Mr. Hamp quietly interjected, as he stood behind the two women. "Can it be?" he asked, staring at Hattie with a puzzled look on his face.

Hattie looked back at him and just nodded her head.

"What are you two talking about?" Dee Dee wanted to know.

"It's Selena Jarrellson Dubois, honey," Hattie whispered to her.

"Who?" Dee Dee asked.

"Selena is a first cousin to Anna Mary," she explained. "She's also the daughter, on paper, anyway, of Raymond Jarrellson, who was a missionary to India. Raymond died from malaria while over there in India, and there was always talk that his wife, Magda, had given birth to a child who was fathered not by Raymond, but by the son of an Indian maharajah."

"Really? So, where does the Dubois come in?" Dee Dee asked her.

"I'm not quite sure, unless it was her real father's

last name," Hattie said. "At this point, who knows? The whole business was kept quiet for such a long time. No one knew for certain until Selena's mother died in Delhi about five years ago."

Hattie explained that just before Raymond's death, he told his brother, Gus, about the child to whom Magda had given birth.

"She was raised in a convent in Calcutta where the family paid regular visits," Hattie continued. "Supposedly, the father of the child, who visited her from time to time, but never chose to acknowledge her, left her a tremendous amount of money as an inheritance. She was later sent to England for finishing school, and since that time has lived with her father's cousin in a home in the Belgravia section of London. Now, here she is," Hattie added, still shaking her head. "Dear, God, they really did not describe her beauty adequately."

Watson had been animatedly talking with Carl Alvin Campbell and laughing while telling him a story about God only knew what. His back was to the staircase, and when Carl Alvin suddenly diverted his attention away from Watson and over to what was going on behind him, Watson also turned to look. His breath seemed to catch in his throat for a few moments when he spotted the beautiful woman coming down the staircase.

Anna Mary, it turned out, had choreographed the entire scene. She was eagerly watching Watson's expression out of the corner of her eye when she took

Selena's hand and kissed her on the cheek. With the ease of one born to privilege, Anna Mary then moved to the microphone underneath the big white tent, held up her hand, and asked for everyone's attention.

"Dear friends and loved ones," she began. "Stanley and I are so pleased you could join us on this happy occasion, as we welcome home our son, Watson. Come here, darling!" she called out, motioning for him to join her.

Watson reluctantly walked over to his mother's side and she kissed his cheek.

"We are also so blessed to have our cousin Selena Jarrellson Dubois join us," Anna Mary went on. "She arrived today from London. So, with open arms, we welcome this beautiful girl for the first time ever to her ancestral home here on the banks of the Suwannee River. Come here, darling!" she shouted a tad too loud.

With the grace of an accomplished dancer, Selena seemed to float over to the microphone. As she did so, it was clear that Watson's heart had skipped a few beats. His face flushed red and his eyes grew wide, and then he smiled at Selena, as if he was drinking in her beauty. His mother greeted Selena and then introduced her to Watson. Before he even hugged his cousin to welcome her, he knew he was attracted to her, bizarre and immoral as it was to be drawn to a blood relative. The attraction, however, was something over which he seemed to have no control.

Just then, the band struck up an old classic tune called "Stardust", made famous by the late Nat King

Cole. Without realizing he was doing it, Watson heard himself ask Selena to dance.

"I'd be delighted, Watson," she replied, in an upper class, British accent that was tinged with a hint of the sing-song cadence of India.

Watson proudly led her out onto the dance floor, as if he was presenting a Westminster show dog. He was so engrossed in staring at her that he was totally unaware that the dance floor had been cleared for the two of them. He also wasn't aware that everyone's eyes were on them as they waltzed to the song.

Watson was so enthralled with the vision of beauty in his arms that he didn't notice his mother's discerning glance as she looked over at his father, either. All he knew at that precise moment, as he breathed in Selena's intoxicating fragrance and felt the softness of her skin, was that he was in love.

Destini could hear the words coming from Watson's mouth as he spoke to Selena.

"How long will you be visiting with us, my dear?" he asked her, as they continued to glide around the dance floor.

"I have no plans to leave anytime in the near future," she replied, smiling at him, as if she was truly enjoying herself. "I want to become better acquainted with my family… and that includes you, Watson. I'm depending on you to make this visit educational and entertaining. You won't fail me, will you?" she coyly asked him.

"No, Miss Selena," he replied, grinning from ear to

ear. "I will not fail you. I promise you."

He didn't fail her, either. Over the next couple of months, Watson was never far from Selena's side. When she eventually told him she was planning on going back to England, as her visit there was coming to an end, he did something a bit wild and crazy... for Watson, that is. He drove over to Continental Planter's Bank and grabbed his grandmother Jarrellson's diamond and platinum engagement ring out of his safety deposit box.

Later, as the two of them lounged on a sandbar near the old Jarrellson farm, their feet dipping into the cool waters of the Suwannee River, Watson proclaimed his love for his third cousin and asked her to marry him.

Without hesitation, she accepted. She explained that never having any truly secure place in the world, nor a real family except for her aunt, she was overjoyed at the proposition of belonging.

Watson knew that marriage to Selena would ensure financial and emotional well-being for him, but he never dreamed that upon receiving both of those things, that he would actually fall in love.

Chapter 6

Meanwhile, still on the private jet to New Orleans, Dee Dee was mindlessly flipping through magazines. She happened to look over at Destini again and noticed she was blinking her eyes and twitching, as if she was about to finally rouse from her sleep. Then, she settled down and was still again… until she spoke.

"Huh? Did she just say flowers?" Dee Dee asked Mark, who was sitting across from her now.

"I didn't hear anything," Mark mumbled, not even bothering to open his eyes. "I'm trying to sleep, Dee Dee. Be quiet, girl."

"Whatever…" Dee Dee grunted, shaking her head. "Looks like I got me a couple of deadbeats here, don't I? Well, except for you, Destini. My goodness, girl, you can do some talkin' in your sleep," she added, chuckling to herself.

It was about an hour before they'd be landing and other than this little twitching episode, and her intermittent mumbling, Destini was showing no signs of awakening. The fact was, Destini really was thinking about flowers in her dream state. She thought of the thousands and thousands of flowers imported for the wedding of Selena Jarrellson Dubois to Watson Jarrellson Williams.

The sanctuary of the small Seraph Springs United Methodist Church was filled to capacity with imported orchids, sweet smelling jasmine, orange blossoms, and roses in shades of pale pink, cream, and white, while tall, thin, white candles burned on gold candelabras around the high altar. The Bishop for the entire United Methodist Diocese of Florida would be conducting the ceremony.

Selena chose two attendants for her wedding; her cousin, Lady Arabella Simpson-Keyes from England, and Dee Dee, whom she had come to favor quite a bit since their first meeting at the welcoming party. The two attendants were dressed in matching pale pink, silk chiffon gowns that evoked a sari-like effect and they were radiant, to say the least.

However, it was the bride who stole the show, as it always is, and rightfully so. She was dressed in an ivory wedding gown that had been worn by her mother-in-law when she married, as well as a point d'esprit Brussels lace heirloom veil that had been used by the Jarrellson brides since before the Civil War. Again, Selena seemed to float on air as she walked down the aisle. Her breathtaking beauty had silenced the entire sanctuary.

As the couple knelt at the altar, which was banked by colorful, fragrant flower arrangements, Anna Mary wept. It wasn't just wedding day tears, either. Those who sat in the pews behind her knew they were tears of relief, or perhaps it was guilt or repentance.

All Anna Mary knew, however, was that her son

was happy, and she seemed to delight in it. She had done her best, as she had promised the Lord at this same altar years ago. She had prayed before the altar every single week that despite their rarified educations and aloof ways, much of what her husband's people were would not rub off on her son.

Now, as the candlelight bathed the sanctuary, Anna Mary looked to the Jarrellson memorial window of Jesus praying in the garden. On so many Sundays, she felt an agony of her own and she identified with that of the Savior himself in that depiction. Now, she felt relief, and for the first time in many years, love flooded her heart and found its way to her eyes.

Destini began to stir in her seat again and she started mumbling quite loud.

"No!" she called out. "Noooo!"

Dee Dee tried patting her arm to awaken her, but all it did was send her back into a deep sleep.

Still dreaming, Destini heard the ringing of a telephone late one afternoon. It was about two years after the wedding and she was at the Williams' home. She heard Anna Mary scream, "Noooo!" and so she ran to her. Crumpled on the floor, Anna Mary was holding the receiver in her hand and she was mumbling incoherently.

Destini grabbed the phone from her and calmly said into the mouthpiece, "Williams' residence."

A proper British voice on the other end said, "I was speaking to Mrs. Stanley Williams. What happened? Is she still there?" the voice asked.

Destini took another look at Anna Mary, who was still wallowing on the floor, and she replied, "At present, she is unable to take your call. May I take a message? I am one of the housekeepers, Destini Wilson."

"Is Mr. Williams at home?" the man on the phone asked.

"No, sir, he is not here at present. May I take a message?" she asked again, wondering what in the world was going on, as she watched Anna Mary sob uncontrollably as she lay on the floor, curled up in the fetal position.

"I suppose so," the man said in a refined English accent, and then he let out a frustrated sigh. "Mr. and Mrs. Watson Williams... do you know them?" he asked her.

"Yes, I do," Destini said. "Known Watson since he was born. Known Miss Selena since they married."

"They are dead," the man bluntly said. "I am an investigator with the London police. They were killed early this morning on the outskirts of London."

"Oh, no... oh, my goodness, no..." Destini muttered, in a state of shock at the moment, and then realizing why Anna Mary was acting the way she was. "They was going to Lady Arabella's for the weekend," she managed to say to the man.

"What?" the officer replied, as if he didn't understand her.

"How did it happen?" Destini asked.

"The weather was quite foggy," he said, sounding

as clinical as an uncaring trauma doctor who had seen one too many violent deaths. "They ran off the road, overcorrected their automobile, and the car turned over. They were killed instantly."

"And their daughter? Miss Mary Selena?" Destini asked.

"The child was not with them," he said. "She had been left in the care of her aunt in London."

"Oh, thank God!" Destini said. "Thank God!"

She asked the investigator to send whatever information he had to the Williams' residence in Seraph Springs and she gave him the address. She also asked that the same information be faxed or sent via overnight mail to Campbell County Sheriff Bartow Lewis.

"Please send it to him," she said, and she gave him the telephone number again. "It would be best for him to relate this information."

About a week-and-a-half later, the funeral for Watson and Selena was held in London. Anna Mary and Stanley flew over there and, surprisingly or not, they decided to bury their son there, rather than ship his body back home to the States.

The funeral turned out to be one of the largest and most sincerely attended in the area. Watson's casket was closed, but Selena's was open and, remarkably, her face and her body looked immaculate, with no signs of injurious trauma whatsoever. She laid full length in a magnificent mahogany casket, dressed in a pale pink evening gown. She looked every inch the great beauty she had always been.

The baby girl, Mary Selena, became an issue after the funeral. Would she become the ward of her paternal grandparents, or would she go to live with her aunt, Lady Arabella, outside of London? It was soon decided by a judge that she would live with Lady Arabella at her country home, but she would visit her paternal grandparents during the summer months. It would be decided by the courts in the United States what further arrangements would be made when the child turned eight years of age.

People, especially Anna Mary and Stanley, were a bit shocked, to say the least, when the last will and testament of Watson and Selena Williams was read aloud in a London attorney's office two days after the funeral. The will clearly stated that Mary Selena would become the ward of Destini Wilson, should anything happen to Stanley and Anna Mary Williams, who would be her legal guardians once the child turned eight years of age. A trust fund, the will stated, had already been established to care for the child.

Destini stirred in her sleep again, but she wasn't ready to wake up yet, as her dream continued. It was now years later and one month before Mary Selena's eighth birthday. Anna Mary and Stanley had decided to challenge a portion of the will and the custody agreements regarding the child. They partially won their case in a court in Jacksonville. However, Destini would remain next in line as legal guardian should Stanley and Anna Mary both die.

The new custody agreement stated that the paternal grandparents would be placing the child in a structured boarding school arrangement throughout the remainder of her elementary and high school years, rather than move in with Stanley and Anna Mary. Having lost one child to the north already, Anna Mary, who wasn't completely heartless about the situation, did much research regarding exclusive boarding schools for girls. She decided upon a Catholic girl's school in New Orleans under the direction of Catholic nuns within the Ursuline order.

Anna Mary then decided she would move to New Orleans, lease a home there, and leave Campbell County and her ancestral home behind, at least until Mary Selena finished her schooling. She settled on what she referred to as a quaint Creole cottage, although, it was more like a mini mansion. It was just a mile from the Ursuline School, and she devoted herself to her granddaughter and her education as best she could. Stanley stayed behind in Florida to continue his work, but he did make several trips to New Orleans.

Mary Selena truly was a beautiful girl with her mother's coloring and her daddy's tall, proud carriage. She was a favorite of the Sisters and the Mother Superior at the Ursuline School, and she excelled both academically and socially. All the girls at the school loved learning about far-away places and they often asked Mary Selena questions about her own mother's native India. She answered as best as she could remember and it was mostly based on things her aunt had told her.

Anna Mary would oftentimes take her granddaughter shopping to a small boutique in New Orleans that catered to the local Hindu Indian population, so that she could purchase saris. One year at Halloween, Mary Selena dressed in a hot pink sari and her makeup was done by one of her schoolmates. When Anna Mary and Stanley saw her in her outfit, they were taken aback at the great beauty standing before them. Both of them, especially Stanley, had come to appreciate how special their granddaughter was. Mary Selena was now their world and their heart, and each day spent with her, they said, was an added blessing.

Chapter 7

Upon landing in New Orleans, Dee Dee reached over and gently shook Destini's arm until she opened her eyes.

"You have taken quite a nap, girl, and evidently dreamed some pretty wild dreams, too," Dee Dee told her.

"Oh… we here?" Destini mumbled, as she rubbed the sleep from her eyes, and stretched her arms and legs.

"Yes, ma'am! The Crescent City, the Big Easy awaits!" Dee Dee said, with a childlike excitement in her voice, which only evoked a huge yawn from Destini, as she stretched her arms over her head again.

Moments later, the two women gathered their bags and donned their sunglasses, and then Mark helped them into their coats, as it was a tad chilly outside. As they walked into the airport terminal, they were greeted by a huge banner decorated with gold and silver glitter. On it was written:

"You're here for a good time! Welcome Destini and Dee Dee!"

Dressed in a beautiful red sweater, a pair of designer jeans, and knee-high black boots, stood none other than Miss Sissy Paquette, who immediately dropped the banner when she spotted her two old friends. Then, she ran to them with outstretched arms, squealing the entire way.

"Welcome to New Orleans, my friends!" Miss Sissy gushed. "Gosh, the two of you are a welcome sight for these tired, old eyes. It's so good to see you," she kept on, and then she tightly hugged both of them.

"Oh, Miss Sissy, you lookin' like a million... no ma'am... make that twenty million dollars!" Destini declared.

"It's the truth, Miss Sissy," Dee Dee agreed. "You look absolutely wonderful. If you're hiding the fountain of youth here in New Orleans, please do let us in on the secret."

"Oh, now, you two girls know flattery will get you everywhere. Oh, well, lookie there. Who is that gorgeous young man standing behind you?" Miss Sissy asked, although she knew exactly who it was. "Mark, my God, honey! I can't believe it! Don't you look handsome in your uniform? Gosh it's good to see you," she added, and she gave Mark a huge Miss Sissy hug, too.

"Good to see you, as well, Miss Sissy," Mark said. "How have you been?"

"Honey, if I was any better there'd be two o' me. I love this town, and so far, it seems to love me, too. Where are you staying, baby? Are you here overnight, or do you have to get back on that plane right away?"

"I'm here until tomorrow morning," Mark replied.

"I'm staying at a place in the French Quarter tonight."

"Correction," Miss Sissy said, waving her finger at him. "You are staying *not far* from the French Quarter. You're going to stay with me tonight, honey. Me and these girls, that is. And don't you worry. I have plenty of room."

"Oh, I wouldn't want to put you out none, Miss Sissy," Mark said.

"Not a bit, honey," she said. "The more the merrier, I say. Ain't that what Mr. Hamp would say about them big Christmas and Thanksgiving gatherings at Camp EZ, Destini? The more the merrier?"

"Yes, ma'am, that's what he always said, and he meant it," Destini replied. "He was so happy when folks would come and bring their families and loads of food, and everyone would talk and enjoy themselves. He was happy most of the time, but especially at them times on the holidays. He loved them," she added, as she retrieved a tissue from her purse to wipe a few tears from her eyes.

"Well, honey, they are wonderful memories and we are going to make some great new ones ourselves, including some that are fun-filled starting right now."

Miss Sissy signaled to one of the baggage attendants to help with the luggage, and the four of them made their way to her roomy, white Cadillac Escalade SUV.

"Oooh, nice ride, Miss Sissy," Destini said.

"Thank you, honey. It was a wonderful gift from the sheriff before I left Campbell County. Bless his heart. How is he?"

"Well, he's a lot more stubborn… and sadder, too, since you left town, Miss Sissy," Destini told her.

"Oh? Does he ever ask about me?"

"I can answer that one," Dee Dee piped up. "I can attest that I have seen him several times talking with Carl Alvin concerning various elements of business we're involved in. There is never a time that he doesn't ask about you or make a comment about you," Dee Dee assured her. "If I may… what happened between you two, Miss Sissy? I know that's a personal question, but we're close enough, I think. So, tell me… what happened between you and the sheriff?"

"Life happened, honey," Miss Sissy said with a frown. "The sheriff, as you may or may not know, has enough money that he's going to live and die in Campbell County in comfort. It's his birth ground. No matter how sad and rundown Turpricone becomes, he'll be just like your aunts, honey. He ain't goin' nowhere."

"You're probably right about that," Dee Dee said.

"As for me, I loved the place I moved to in the late sixties," Miss Sissy said. "I loved it until the last five years I was there and then I didn't love it anymore. It got too hard, sweetheart. Much too hard," she explained.

"I know what you mean," Dee Dee said.

"The population kept going down, the businesses kept closing, the schools were struggling, and all around me was depression. It was just awful. No wonder Campbell County has one of the highest rates of not only obesity, but suicide, as well, from what I've been reading lately."

"Again, you are spot on, Miss Sissy," Dee Dee said.

"The liquor store does a booming business, still, I'll betcha, and do you know who their largest clientele is?" Miss Sissy asked. "The young people, for sure. Now, if you ask me, that's what's really sad, my dear. I know I'm talking hard and maybe even mean about your hometown, but you have to remember, it wasn't my home."

"Yeah, I realize that, Miss Sissy," Dee Dee said.

"You see, my hometown went through what Campbell County is going through a lot sooner," Miss Sissy went on. "I was raised in the Mississippi Delta, remember? My daddy worked like a mule on one of them big cotton plantations as a manager of the place. It was several thousand acres and several hundred people when I was a young girl. Then came the mechanization and the field workers moved someplace else because there was no longer any work. The man who owned the place kept my daddy on simply out of honor. Meanwhile, Mama kept working at the school cafeteria, and with the help of the principal, God rest Mr. Morris Carson's soul, I was able to get a small scholarship to a local vocational school and earned my cosmetology license."

Miss Sissy continued yammering away as she drove the girls. It was as if she had just emerged from a thirty-year solitary prison confinement and simply needed to hear herself speak, Destini thought, although, she always enjoyed listening to her stories.

"I won't ever forget the first time I went to New Orleans on one of them cosmetology conferences," Missy Sissy kept on. "I had never been further from Jackson, Mississippi than to travel to Memphis once when my great aunt died. I was seventeen-years-old, just days before my eighteenth birthday. When I came to New Orleans that spring of nineteen hundred and... well, you know... a long time ago, I vowed that I would return and work there, and rarely go back to the Delta except to visit with Daddy and Mama. I did just that, too."

"What happened next?" Destini asked.

"Well, from there, because my sister had moved to Turpricone and my niece, Lollie, was there, I moved there and started working at Betty's Beauty Box, which back then was owned by Miss Agnes Lee. I eventually bought her out and had some great years there, except for the last five, which were a struggle just to make ends meet. Plus, my sister remarried and moved back to Mississippi, and Lollie was off doing her own thing."

"I remember those days," Destini said.

"When it got to where I wasn't even making utility money to stay open, it was time to shut down. Poor Campbell County," Miss Sissy continued. "I know y'all love it there, but y'all are in a unique situation. Your money is made and your future is secure, and that's the same for about fifteen percent of the county. The rest of 'em are sadder than the Mississippi Delta I left so many years ago, and that is the really, really sad part."

"Wow, you know, I guess I never really thought about it in that way before," Dee Dee admitted. "You're absolutely right, though. It is sad."

"Well, life goes on and now I'm back in New Orleans." Miss Sissy said. "It seems I have traveled full circle," she added with a heavy sigh. "I'm a cosmetologist at the same location where I started over fifty years ago. Thank God, I'm still able to work about three days a week. When I returned, you'd be surprised how many folks came in and booked appointments. It's a joy. It's a blessing."

"Yes, it is," Destini said. "Yes, indeed, it is."

"My daddy's sister, Aunt Isabel, died about five years ago," Miss Sissy continued. "She worked her whole life as the chief paralegal for a big law firm here in New Orleans. She had no children, so I stayed in touch with her. When she died, she left me her spacious two-story cottage at the edge of the Garden district and enough money that, with what I saved… well, I ain't Howard Hughes, but if I'm careful, I can live comfortably until I kick that final bucket. I always live with joy, too."

Dee Dee glanced over at Destini and winked at her.

"Let me ask you something, Miss Sissy," Dee Dee interrupted her. "Has New Orleans offered you anything in the way of, umm… you know… male companionship? You know… something to provide a balm for your scarred ol' heart."

Miss Sissy doubled over in laughter at the blunt question and came close to running off the road.

Then, she said, "One thing about Miss Sissy. I don't kiss and tell. Never have and never will. Let's just say there's a difference between being lonely and being alone. If I'm alone, my dears, it is by choice. However… Miss Sissy is never lonely," she added, still laughing.

As always, Miss Sissy had a way about her that never failed to entertain, as both Dee Dee and Destini cracked up laughing, too.

Chapter 8

Miss Sissy was still gabbing a mile a minute when the group finally arrived at their destination, leaving little opportunity for anyone else to say much at all, but no one was complaining. Miss Sissy was now and always had been a downright joy to listen to. She seemed to have a bottomless vault of stories to choose from, too.

"Well, here we are," Miss Sissy said, drawing in a deep breath as she pulled up to her cottage and shut off the engine. "I have a young man here who helps sweep up at our shop, so he'll be helping to take in your luggage. I give him free room and board and it has worked out well for both of us." With that, she yelled out, "Justin! Justin, come out here and meet my friends and help Miss Sissy!"

When Justin emerged onto the front steps, Destini and Dee Dee both let out audible gasps and it was obvious they were more than impressed with what they were looking at. Justin was about six feet tall, weighed probably around one-hundred-ninety-five pounds, and all of it was distributed in just the right places. He had dark café au lait-colored skin and eyes as green as a lush forest. To say the least, he was quite a stunning male specimen. He immediately bounded down the steps like a graceful cheetah and went over to pick up Dee Dee's bag.

"Why, thank you, Justin," Dee Dee said, blushing. "May an older lady from the Sunshine State compliment you on being a very handsome young man?"

"Thank you, ma'am," he said, blushing redder than Dee Dee now, as he lowered his eyes. "You don't look that old, though," he added, which earned him a pat on the back from Dee Dee.

"Oh, my word, I don't think I have ever seen such long, beautiful, dark eyelashes on anyone before... male or female," Dee Dee complimented him.

"Now, don't you be flirtin' with this boy and gettin' him all turned around," Miss Sissy warned Dee Dee. "He's in college here over at Tulane and he's serious about his studies. He does a good job for us down at the shop, too. His mama is a school nurse at one of the elementary schools not far from here, and she raised Justin by herself with the help of his great-aunt."

"I'm impressed," Dee Dee said, still ogling him. "Looks like your mama did one fine job of raising you."

"He's a good driver, too, so he's going to chauffer us around to different places, but first, y'all come inside and get settled," Miss Sissy said. "I have cool beverages, some tasty little canapés and other munchies waiting for us. Whadya say let's start our own little hurricane party and sip on a couple of them while we reminisce. How's that sound?" she asked the girls.

"I'm in," Dee Dee said.

"Me, too," Destini chimed in.

The three ladies, along with Justin and Mark, enjoyed a wonderful couple of hours visiting together. Destini told Miss Sissy all about her daughter, Bunnye, and how she was getting along. She told her about her brother and sister-in-law, Duke and Essie, and about them building their new house. She also told her she had to hire one of her cousins, who was a licensed practical nurse, to look after Mama Tee because of her frail health.

"Her mind is still sharp as a tack, though," Destini assured everyone.

"Well, Mama Tee could always see more as a blind woman than most people could with two eyes and twenty-twenty vision," Miss Sissy said with a smile.

Dee Dee started to tell Miss Sissy about Carl Alvin and her Aunt Hattie, but Miss Sissy waved her off and said, "We've got plenty of time to hear about them, honey. What Miss Sissy wants to know is how the Cuban American Prince, Señor Fernandez is? That's what I really want to know. So… how is he?"

"Ooooh, Miss Sissy," Destini said, laughing. "You ain't changed a bit."

"I hope not, sweetie," Miss Sissy said, laughing along with her. "Oh, and thank you for saying that," she added. "I take great pride in the fact that I do my best to keep myself from changing as little as I possibly can. Now, tell me about your fiancé, Dee Dee, and tell me about the wedding plans. There are wedding plans, right?" she asked.

"We've talked about it," Dee Dee said, quite nonchalantly, as she sipped on her Miss Sissy Special Hurricane Cocktail. "Right now, though, we haven't made any definite decisions. Aunt Hattie is upset because I'm in the process of converting to Catholicism. It seems to mean a lot to Ricardo and I love him, so I'm doing it. Even though I went to the Methodist church when I was growing up, our family wasn't a particularly religious family."

"Your mama and daddy, and Mr. Hamp might not have been, but let me tell you something," Destini butted in. "Your Aunt Hattie was the pillar of that Methodist church in Turpricone and I know she ain't gonna give up on you marrying there without a fight."

"Believe me, honey, she has spoken her piece already. That's for sure," Dee Dee said. "I'm truly thinking about asking you, Destini, if we can get married at Camp EZ."

"What?!" Destini shouted. "Girl, you know you can! Let me hug your neck!" Just seconds later, Destini had an epiphany. "I think we need to wait until next year, though, right before Thanksgiving," she told Dee Dee. "We can have the wedding then. With the leaves turning colors and everything just a little crispy... pretty Thanksgiving decorations all around, and fall colors... yes, ma'am!"

"I got one better for you than that," Dee Dee said. "I was thinking of getting married *on* Thanksgiving, you know... the morning of Thanksgiving, next year, of course, and then inviting everyone to participate in the Thanksgiving feast at Camp EZ as part of the reception."

"Now, I like that idea," Destini said, and she hugged Dee Dee. Then she looked at her with tears in her eyes. "I know who you thinking of, girl," she said. "You ain't gotta say. I just know it."

"You're right. Yes, I have thought a lot about it," Dee Dee admitted, as a lone tear fell from her eye. Then, she perked up again. "I'm going to have a beautiful gown in which to marry, and I want you, the girls, and Miss Sissy here to stand up with me."

"Me!" Miss Sissy exclaimed. "Oh, Lord have mercy, girl! You know I would be honored!"

"What we goin' wear?" Destini asked.

"I will let you girls sort that out," Dee Dee said. "I was thinking something street-length, even fancy suits in fall colors like purple, gold, deep green, rust, deep maroon, orange, or even bronze. Think jewel tones."

At that moment, Justin, who had been sitting off to the side chatting with Mark, got up to refresh everyone's drinks.

"Oh, and you, Justin... handsome, handsome Justin, I want you to come to the wedding, too, honey," Dee Dee offered. "You can come with Miss Sissy. I'm sure she won't mind. I can guarantee you when those girls way down upon the Suwannee River get a look at you, they'll go ape doodoo."

"Sho' will," Destini agreed. "I might act a little apish myself. Be after yo pretty behind like white on rice. How fast can you run, boy? Them Suwannee River gals can move," she added, laughing.

Justin laughed, too. "Well, yes, I would love to come to your wedding, Miss Dee Dee, on one condition."

Dee Dee looked at Destini and winked, and then she turned to look at Justin. "What condition would that be, Mr. Tall, Dark and Handsome?"

"That I be allowed to bring all the fixins' for a huge pot of Louisiana gumbo and cook it in honor of your Thanksgiving feast," he said.

"Did you hear that, Dee Dee?" Destini gasped. "Did you hear that? Now that's about the sweetest thing I have *ever* heard, and I can answer for her, baby," she added, looking straight into Justin's mesmerizing green eyes. "Yes, you can!"

"Uhhh… excuse me," Mark interjected. "Aren't y'all forgetting somebody?"

"Hmmm… I don't think so," Dee Dee said, scrunching up her face, as if she was wracking her brain trying to remember whom she might have forgotten.

"I think he be talkin' 'bout hisself," Destini whispered to her, although, it was loud enough for everyone else to hear.

"Ya think?" Dee Dee asked, grinning. "You know, Mark," she began. "I really thought you were smarter than that. If any of us is havin' a party or a weddin' or any kind of get together, you are automatically invited, and you're at the top of the invitation list, silly boy."

"Aww, I knew that," Mark said. "It would be nice

to be asked, though."

"Well, consider yourself asked," Dee Dee said, and she reached over to hug him. "I do hope you can make it, too."

"Oh, I'll be there," he said. "I will definitely be there."

"Oh, won't we have fun?" Miss Sissy cooed. "I can hardly wait, but, first, girls, let's take some time and change now. We've got reservations at a wonderful New Orleans restaurant for dinner, and then we're going to listen to some of the best jazz and Dixieland music you girls have ever heard. Y'all go and take a little nap now, if you want. Then, we'll all get ready and we'll leave about eight, okay? While y'all rest, I'm going to call Hortense Gobichaux, my friend who does special design work. She's a finished seamstress and tailor, so I'll get her to do a few drawings for some possible dresses to be used for Dee Dee's wedding. How does that sound?" she asked.

"Does she do custom work on wedding gowns, Miss Sissy?" Dee Dee inquired. "The reason I ask is Aunt Hattie is dying for me to wear her wedding dress. It was custom made for her in Charleston many years ago, and she's had it professionally sealed and stored all these years. She used to have a lady over in Jacksonville, who has been dead now for close to twenty years, "go over that dress", as she called it."

"I can't wait to see it," Miss Sissy said.

"I really want to wear it," Dee Dee said. "It's a beautiful gown, but I know it will need work. I'd also like her to take a look at the Jarrellson veil. While I'm in town, I'll be going by to see Anna Mary. She has the veil here with her. I understand it was first worn by a Jarrellson bride in the late eighteen-forties, not long after the very first sanctuary was built... you know, the Methodist Church in Seraph Springs. The lace of the veil was handmade by nuns over in Belgium, according to my aunt, and it's a very rare fabric. Both the dress and the veil are now kind of a soft ivory color. The veil drops into a train at the back, which is several feet long, and it's absolutely gorgeous. I'd really like to wear both the dress and the veil. In fact, I'm determined to do so."

"Well, Miss Hortense is your gal, honey," Miss Sissy told her. "I don't know exactly how many heirloom gowns and veils she's brought back to life for girls all over Louisiana, Mississippi, Arkansas and Texas, but it's a lot. Her work is not inexpensive, but when she finishes, you can darn sure put on a pair of glasses as thick as you please, and you'll never find one flaw. She does exquisite work, which is why I'm phoning her now about the bridesmaids' dresses. I have something in mind as to the design. I want to talk with Destini, though, and then have her get in touch with the girls or fax a copy of the drawings to them while y'all are here."

"I am truly excited to learn more about Ms. Gobichaux," Dee Dee said. "I wonder if we could get her to come to Seraph Springs for the final fittings and then be there the week before the wedding."

"Honey, with enough money, anything is possible," Miss Sissy told her.

"Money is no object," Dee Dee said. "Gosh, didn't that sound pretentious? Anyway, in this case it isn't. I plan on going to the altar in marriage one time in my life, and I want it to be done beautifully and perfectly."

"Before you go and rest, Dee Dee, I must ask one thing," Destini interjected. "Did I hear you say you were going by Mrs. Anna Mary Williams' house while you're here?"

"Yes, ma'am, I am. I want to see the veil and talk with her about making arrangements to get it to Miss Gobichaux if we decide to go in that direction, and it sounds like we might."

"I want to go with you when you go see her," Destini said.

"You do? Now, that surprises me," Dee Dee said, and then she looked at Miss Sissy and winked.

"Might surprise you, but the visit ain't about her. It's about that baby of Watson's," Destini explained. "That baby is in school here in New Orleans, and I want to see her if they'll let me, if only for a few minutes. I want her to know someone who knew her daddy and who loved him till the day he was killed."

"Well, when I phone Anna Mary, I will ask, Destini, but you know how funny she and Stanley are, and if they say no?" Dee Dee asked, raising her eyebrows.

"Then, it be no," Destini said. "It be no for now, but she goin' grow up one day, and when she do, I will still be where I am, Lord willing, and I will find that chil' and talk to her. I'll be happy to talk with her with Mrs. Anna Mary and Mr. Stanley present. I'm not goin' tell that chil' a thing to upset her, but I do have some photos and some memories that might interest her. She what, about twelve now? She old enough to understand what I will share with her. Ain't nothin' bad. 'Sides, I know what that last will said that Watson wrote. Anything happen to Mr. Stanley and Mrs. Anna Mary, then Mary Selena come to me," she declared. "I got a copy of that will in the safe at Camp EZ, and I takes it out and reads it once in a while. Helps me remember my first baby. I loved him, and he knew I loved him. No doubt about that. He went to his grave knowing that Destini Wilson loved him."

Tears were now flowing down Destini's cheeks, which made everyone else tear up, too.

"Nobody know the memories I have of that time," Destini explained. "Nobody know all I know about that situation. Nobody know but the good Lord himself and blessed Mama Tee and Mr. Hamp. The pain I held in my heart, the prayers I prayed, beggin' the merciful Lord to help that chil'. I can tell all y'all, I gots enough of Mama Tee in me that unless the death angel strikes me down, I will see that baby girl and talk to her in this lifetime. I been praying 'bout it."

Destini pulled out a tissue from her pocketbook and dabbed at her tear-filled eyes, while around her was dead silence.

"Knew the Williams' was here for Mary Selena to

go to school," Destini continued. "Gotta say, Mr. Stanley and Mrs. Anna Mary learned a little somethin' from their experience with Watson. Shipped him off up north to them cold Williams' folk in Massachusetts. I could smell an alligator when I saw both o' dem with dem beady little eyes and that ol' pale skin, with teefs like alligators, and blood that run as cold as one. Yes, ma'am, I sized 'em up the first time I ever seen 'em. They was somethin' else, you hear me? Her wearin' only dark blue or black or grey all the time. Even when she came down when Mrs. Anna Mary held that baby's christenin' that year on Palm Sunday, and everyone there dressed in pretty spring colors and hats, and she come paradin' in the church dressed in an old black dress with a grey and white printed coat over it, and an old black hat. Looked like she goin' mourn over somethin'."

Dee Dee and Miss Sissy had been trying not to laugh, but it wasn't working, as they now had tears streaming down their cheeks, they were laughing so hard.

"I'm serious!" Destini yelled. "Dee Dee, I won't never forget as long as I live, 'cause your Aunt Hattie, your Aunt Nanny and Mr. Hamp look dat Yankee woman over... you notice I ain't said lady, 'cause in my opinion, she wasn't one, but they looked her over good. I remember Miss Nanny asked, "Honey, did you think we were burying someone here today? Did you get your wires crossed?" So, the old woman said, "You know, this came from one of Boston's finest

department stores." And your Aunt Nanny says, "And
I bet you bought it out de basement of dat store."
Needless to say, her gator mouf bared them old, mean
looking teef. Looked kinda like an old Boston bulldog
about to growl and bite someone."

Now, everyone in the room was laughing out loud.

"Oh, Destini. You are so funny," Dee Dee said,
still laughing. "I can just hear Aunt Nanny saying all
those things."

"Yes, indeed," Destini said. "Oh, she was
somethin' else, all right. I thought for sure we was goin'
fight another Civil War startin' right there in Seraph
Springs. Needless to say, them two ladies gave each
other a wide berth at the brunch followin' the
reception."

"I'm sure they did," Dee Dee said, as she dabbed at
her face with a tissue.

"Then, Mr. Stanley and Mrs. Anna Mary sent dat
baby off to live up there with dem folks," Destini
concluded. "It's a wonder he wasn't more ruined than
he was."

Chapter 9

"Well, we all have our glad rags on! Let's go out and party!" Miss Sissy shouted.

It was just about to strike eight o'clock in the evening and everyone was dressed to the nines for a night out on the town. With Justin behind the wheel and Mark sitting across from him, the three ladies chit-chatted the entire way over to a marvelous Creole restaurant in the center of New Orleans. It came highly recommended by both Miss Sissy and Justin. It turned into a long, long dinner, filled with jokes, laughter, and enough reminiscing to last a lifetime. Plus, there was enough food to feed Pharaoh's army and everything was absolutely delicious.

During dinner, Destini told Miss Sissy she had caught a lot of crawfish in her day, but until tonight she had never eaten one. She had everyone in stitches when she looked at the Crawfish Etouffee and announced, "Lawd! Nevuh thought I'd eat fish bait, but here goes!"

They all had a good laugh, too, when Justin nearly jumped out of his chair when the waiter, who was standing right behind him, ignited the Bananas Foster. Later, Dee Dee commented that the coffee they were served came as close to being as tasty and delicious as the coffee served at Camp EZ.

Destini raised her eyebrows and remarked, "You said *almost*, didn't you, Dee Dee?"

"Yes," Dee Dee said. "Almost, but not quite."

"Damn right," Destini mumbled.

At the end of the meal, the happy group walked the two blocks over to a small jazz club where they enjoyed outstanding music and even more socializing for a good two hours.

Inside, the club was dimly lit, almost pitch black, in fact, and the air was heavy with cigarette and cigar smoke. It was almost like stepping back in time to the Roaring Twenties, Destini thought, as she recalled a few old classic movie musicals she had seen over the years, such as *Cabaret* and *Bugsy Malone.*

The faint lighting around the circumference of the stage was casting a purplish glow across the crowd, distorting people's faces. If the music hadn't been so upbeat, it would have been downright spooky, she thought.

She happened to look across the room and thought she saw Anna Mary and Stanley standing by the front entrance, but she shook it off as a figment of her imagination or too much smoke in her eyes. When she looked again, the couple had vanished.

As she sat absently stirring her cocktail, she asked Miss Sissy if she knew the club's manager. Miss Sissy said she did and she motioned one of the cocktail waitresses over to the table. Destini handed the girl a twenty dollar bill and told her what she wanted. In less than three minutes, the waitress brought the manager over to the table.

"Good evening, ladies and gentleman. Is everything all right here?" he asked.

"Everything's perfect," Destini said. "I have a question for you, though. That well-dressed man and his lady who left here a few minutes ago... do you know who they were?"

"Yes, ma'am," he said, smiling. "That's Mr. and Mrs. Williams. They come in here about twice a week. They never have more than a couple of drinks. She always has two champagne cocktails and he drinks bourbon and water."

"Thank you," Destini said to him. "Oh, and please thank the wonderful staff you have here, as well as the musicians. I am thoroughly enjoying my evening."

"You are quite welcome, ma'am," he said, smiling from ear to ear. "Have a good evening," he added. "What's left of it, that is. We'll be closing in about ten minutes."

Moments later, the ladies collected their purses, shawls and jackets, and headed for the exit with Justin and Mark steps behind them. Once outside, they leisurely walked to where the car was parked about two blocks away along the curb. A light, misty fog had begun to roll in off the Mississippi River and the air was thick and humid. Dee Dee remarked that the city looked as if it had been covered in a grey tulle fabric.

The drive home included more chatter about the evening, how good the food was, as well as the club, and all the fun everyone had. Once back at Miss Sissy's place, Destini, Dee Dee and Mark all thanked their hostess for a fabulous evening, and then thanked Justin for being the designated driver. Then it was lights out for everyone.

Dee Dee and Destini shared the larger of the two vacant guestrooms that had two queen-sized beds, and Mark settled into the smaller guestroom across the hall from them, while Justin settled into his apartment above the garage.

After changing into her nightgown, Destini plopped onto her bed and let out a pleasurable moan as her head sunk into a comfortable down pillow that was inside a white, satin pillowcase. Her eyes were wide open, though, as she thought about Watson, his daughter and his parents, and how they had been interwoven in her life.

After a while, she did fall asleep, and in her dreams that night she saw Watson's little girl, Mary Selena. She imagined what she might look like right now. About an hour later, she was awakened by Dee Dee, who told her she was acting extremely restless in her sleep.

"You were mumbling something about the river and Uncle Hamp," Dee Dee said.

"Yeah, you're right," Destini said, barely above a whisper, as she wiped her eyes. "I believe I *was* dreaming about that."

"Well, go back to sleep, but this time be a little quieter, willya?" Dee Dee teased her.

"Yes, ma'am," Destini said, and then she turned over on her side and drifted back to sleep.

Immediately, she started dreaming again. This time, she saw Mary Selena at age six. It was early spring and she and Mama Tee had taken a rare excursion to their favorite fishing spot on the bank of the Suwannee River about a mile away from Mama Tee's place. Mr. Hamp had graciously arranged for the transportation that day, as well as all of Mama Tee's comforts.

"I hear somethin' up there, high on the river bank," Mama Tee whispered to Destini shortly after they arrived. "You hear dat rustlin'?" she asked her. "Somebody up on dat bank. Ain't no animal makin' dat kind o' fuss."

Destini crept up the steep bank of the river and soon spotted a young girl dressed in a simple blue-flowered sundress and a pair of white sneakers. One look at her face and she immediately knew who the little girl was. She seemed completely engrossed in picking violets, one right after the other. Destini didn't want to startle her or scare her off, but she simply had to say hello to her. She inched closer and closer until she was about three feet away from her, partially hidden behind a large cypress tree.

"Them's pretty flowers, honey," she softly said to the young girl.

The child jumped, but she didn't appear to be frightened by Destini.

"Who are you? Do I know you?" she asked.

"No, honey, but I know you," Destini told her. "I knew your daddy when he was your age. Took care of him, I did."

"Oh! You're the one in the framed photograph I have by my bed!" the girl exclaimed, as her eyes widened. "You're Destini, aren't you?"

"Why, yes, I am," Destini said, smiling. She was so happy that the girl actually knew who she was. "And what is your name?" she asked.

"I'm Mary Selena," she told her.

"Oh, that's such a pretty name," Destini said, and the little girl smiled.

Without warning, Mary Selena rushed toward her with no hesitation whatsoever. Destini opened her arms and Mary Selena fell into them. Then, she embraced the little girl, as if she was loving on her own daughter.

"Sweet angel," Destini whispered to her.

"My father loved you," Mary Selena said.

"Oh, honey, I loved him, too… and I love you. I never laid eyes on you until today, but I love you just the same, and I have prayed for you."

"We're leaving next week," Mary Selena told her, as a frown spread across her face. "I don't want to go, but we're leaving to go to New Orleans and live there for a while. I'll be going to school there. It's a nice school, my grandma told me. She said we weren't going up north where it's cold. She said we were staying in the South and that the school in New Orleans has nice teachers."

"I'm sure it does, baby," Destini said, as her eyes filled with tears. "Give me another hug, sweetheart, and then you go on back to your folks. Just know I'll be praying for you all the time."

"Thank you, Miss Destini," Mary Selena said, smiling again. "I'll be praying for you, too."

Destini kept drifting in and out of slumber until she reached a zone halfway between awake and asleep. That's when she whispered a prayer for Mary Selena and vowed that she would go to see her before leaving New Orleans.

Chapter 10

The next morning began with Café au Lait and a special treat of mouthwatering Beignets, a deep-fried pastry that Destini couldn't stop raving about. Miss Sissy had even brought out her finest china to serve it all.

Everyone was having a grand time, laughing and talking, while the compliments kept pouring in about the entire breakfast Miss Sissy and Justin had prepared. Mark had ducked out before sunrise and hailed a taxi, so he could catch an early flight to his next exotic destination. He had hinted the previous day that it might be somewhere in the Caribbean with a well-known, but unnamed celebrity.

After the breakfast dishes were washed, dried and put away, with everyone doing their fair share, Miss Sissy announced, "Okay, people! It's time to go shopping! We'll do a little sightseeing, too, so I hope y'all got on your comfortable shoes," she added.

It was coming up on ten o'clock by the time they made it into town. The ladies shopped in some of the most unusual and chic boutiques. Their adventure also included a stop by Madame Hortense's exclusive design boutique. Dee Dee, Destini and Miss Sissy looked at dozens of patterns and fabrics for the bridesmaids' dresses before settling on one that Dee Dee absolutely fell in love with.

Madame Hortense asked Dee Dee to come back to New Orleans within the month with her wedding gown and veil, and then she would show her the preliminary drawings of the dresses for the attendants. It was agreed that on the next trip, Nadine and Wanda Faye would come with her, along with Destini and Miss Sissy.

Dee Dee explained to Miss Sissy that for all of them to stay at her place would be too much trouble, and, in truth, Miss Sissy looked relieved. She did say, however, that she would book reservations for the girls at an exclusive hotel in the French Quarter later that evening.

"It's only a few blocks from my cottage, so it will be convenient enough," Miss Sissy told her.

"Works for me," Dee Dee said.

After they left Ms. Hortense's shop, the group enjoyed a late lunch at a quaint little restaurant/grocery store called Table for Two. There they feasted on Muffaletta sandwiches, a popular choice of the Italian immigrants in the area, Miss Sissy explained.

"You know, I don't think there's any type of food here in New Orleans that I don't like," Destini said. "I especially like the pickle relish. Yum…"

"This homemade gumbo isn't so bad, either," Dee Dee piped up.

As they sat underneath an umbrella-covered patio table outside the restaurant enjoying their lunch,

Destini happened to look across the street and spotted something unusually charming that caught her eye.

"That's a very pretty church," she said to Miss Sissy, as she pointed to it.

"Yes, it is, honey," Miss Sissy agreed.

"The gardens are somethin' else, too. Really nice, and so colorful," Destini continued.

"It's beautiful, isn't it?" Miss Sissy rhetorically asked. "It looks that way year round, too. That church is actually the Ursuline Academy and those little girls just love playing in the gardens. The upper school is on the other side. Some of the girls board there and others are just day students, from what I've been told."

"Uh-huh, sho' is a pretty building," Destini said, slowly nodding her head. "Very nice. I'll bet there ain't many po' girls goin' to school there."

"Actually, you'd be surprised," Miss Sissy replied. "The Order makes an effort to present a student body that is socio-economically and racially diverse. At least, that's what I've been told."

"Well, that's good," Destini said. "Yep, that's real good."

The wheels were definitely turning in Destini's head and no one knew what was going on except maybe Dee Dee, who raised her eyebrows without looking Destini's way. She said nothing, though.

It was a little after two in the afternoon when they were winding down their lunch break. After she took the last bite of her sandwich, Dee Dee asked Miss Sissy if they might go home and rest a bit before going out that night.

"Sure thing, honey," Miss Sissy said. "It'll give Justin time to take care of some errands for me before getting all cleaned up for another night out with the old ladies."

Justin shook his head and laughed. "Some of the most beautiful ladies in the Crescent City, I might add," he said. "I am honored to be your trusted servant."

"Charm will get you everywhere, handsome," Dee Dee said, fluttering her eyelashes at him, which made him blush as red as Miss Sissy's lipstick.

Chapter 11

Once they arrived back at Miss Sissy's home, Dee Dee and Destini went upstairs, while Miss Sissy attended to some shop business. Dee Dee switched on the television and turned the volume down low before lying down on her bed. Meanwhile, Destini wasted no time getting undressed, throwing on a nightgown, and plopping down on the other bed. Not long after her head hit the pillow, she was out like a light… off into dreamland moments later.

"My God, that girl can sleep," Dee Dee said, shaking her head.

This time, Destini dreamed about her second cherished baby after leaving the employment of the Williams'. It was the summer she turned twenty, and she went to work for the Brainard family in neighboring Turpricone to care for their only child.

The Brainards were part of the executive crowd who had moved into the county in the mid-sixties when the phosphate industry came in. Mr. Phillip Julius Brainard Sr. was the president of the company, and his wife, Julie, born and raised in a small town in the Midwest, was definitely an "out of town" girl in Turpricone.

Julie's father owned an automobile dealership in a

small town in Indiana where she grew up. She had been a popular kid in school and held the title of head majorette, as well as homecoming queen. She turned into a pretty lady, and her husband was an extremely handsome man.

Neither of them, it seemed, could ever quite figure out how they managed to spawn, for lack of a better word, such an ugly duckling, but their little Phil was just that. He was shaped like a square with short bandy legs and no neck. He was, quite frankly, a fat child. There was no other way to put it, and he remained husky throughout his early childhood.

Remembering Phil made Destini smile in her sleep. Visits from his Brainard or Miller cousins always pointed to the stark difference between him and them. Destini just figured the child must be some kind of genetic fluke. The cousins were tall, blonde and fair, and most of them had clear, sparkling blue eyes. Phil, on the other hand, had the eyes of a bull terrier. They were beady eyes without much expression at all.

Not long after she was hired to serve as the child's nurse/nanny, it dawned on Destini that she had a situation somewhat similar to the one she faced with Watson Williams, but there were some differences. Little Phil was a lonely child, and one in which his parents didn't have much interest. As much disdain as they had for their son, he was actually quite a brilliant child.

Destini watched in awe as he basically taught himself how to read, beginning at about age three and onward. She watched with pride when after a few piano lessons, he moved right on to the third and fourth year books. She watched him devour information from the company reports his father brought home. She even went to the elementary school with his mother where they learned from the guidance counselor that the child had an IQ that was way beyond anything they had ever witnessed.

Destini felt as if she had never met a more thoughtful child; one who tried so hard to please. He would clean his room to the point that it turned into a compulsion. He'd also clean his father's car on the weekends until it shone like new money.

At the Catholic Church where the family worshipped, the child mastered the catechism so quickly that the priest, Father Corey, related to the parents that they should consider sending the boy to a prestigious boarding school in Chattanooga, Tennessee, which had an excellent academic reputation.

Destini recalled crying when young Phil left to go to that school, but he wrote her on a regular basis. She never failed to send him birthday cards, and he never failed to visit with her when he came home.

The boy graduated valedictorian of his graduating class at the age of sixteen. Then, he attended and graduated from Duke University in Durham, North Carolina, where he received his undergraduate degree. He was awarded a Rhodes scholarship and studied in England for a year. During that time, he traveled extensively throughout the United Kingdom and other parts of Europe, and always made sure to send cards or postcards to Destini from each place he visited.

When he returned to the United States, he enrolled in a prestigious law program at Georgetown Law School in Washington, D.C. He became an expert in the area of environmental law, particularly in regards to agricultural farming and fertilizers, and its effect on groundwater supply and quality. He was frequently called as an expert witness by the federal government, and was engaged to handle some of the most well-known cases affecting the environment across the country.

While in Washington, he married, and he and his wife had a little girl. He had invited Destini to visit a number of times. He also invited Dee Dee, and their friends Nadine and Wanda Faye. Thus far, none of them had been able to pay a visit, though. When he came home at holiday time, he always, without fail, visited them.

After about an hour of dreamy sleep, Destini began to stir from her nap and then she sat upright in the bed, wiping her eyes. Dee Dee was still awake watching *The Late Show* on TV.

"So, what was your dream about this time?" Dee Dee asked her.

Destini smiled and said, "Dreamin' 'bout one of my babies. You remember Phil Brainard?"

"Of course, I remember him," Dee Dee said. "How could I forget him? He loved you so, and was that boy smart? He was so smart. Remember how we would take him with us to Jacksonville on shopping trips, and at the age of seven or eight he knew every street in the city? He was so kind, too, and always so thoughtful."

"Still is," Destini said. "He hasn't forgotten you, either."

"Really?!" Dee Dee exclaimed. "Oh, do tell."

"Well, he wrote me a week or two ago and said he learned you were getting married soon. He asked if he could host a pre-nuptial party for you."

"Oh, my goodness," Dee Dee said. "Oh, don't you just love that little Phil? He's such a sweetheart."

"Yes, he is," Destini said. "You know my baby is a big shot lawyer up in D.C., right? He's called on all the time by the government to testify in major cases concerning the environment. I'm sure that makes his daddy happy."

"I'm sure it doesn't!" Dee Dee countered. "Word around town is that he's now part of a major investigation into the farming industry back home and the effects of all that fertilizer and those toxic pesticides on the groundwater supply."

"Well, whadya know? His daddy might actually sit up and take notice now, won't he?" Destini rhetorically asked, as a wide grin spread across her face.

Chapter 12

Over the next several days, the ladies continued to enjoy their time with Miss Sissy. They shopped, ate at some of the finest restaurants in New Orleans, and purchased Christmas gifts for everyone back home.

For their last night in New Orleans, the ladies dressed up in their most fashionable gowns for another night out on the town. Dinner reservations were made at one of the finest and oldest Creole restaurants in the area. It was while everyone was commenting on the sumptuous mango-flavored sherbet, which was served between courses to cleanse the palette, that Dee Dee spotted Anna Mary and Stanley being escorted to a table on the other side of the room.

"We'll be back in a few minutes," Dee Dee abruptly told Miss Sissy and Justin.

"I doubt that, but y'all go ahead," Miss Sissy said. "If you're not back in five minutes, though, don't expect your dessert to be waitin' on ya," she added with a wicked grin.

"Oh, now, don't do anything rash, Miss Sissy," Dee Dee said. "We'll only be a few minutes."

Never one to be the least bit shy, Dee Dee grabbed an unsuspecting Destini by the arm and the two of them walked over to the table where the Williams couple had just been seated.

Then, with an exuberance that only Dee Dee could project, she declared, "Well, imagine seeing homefolks here! Anna Mary, Stanley, it's good to see you! How are you?"

Anna Mary, who was descended from generations of well-bred Southern ladies, never missed a beat and invited the ladies to sit down with her, while Stanley seemed more than a bit flustered. Destini, who had worked in their home off and on for about ten years, immediately noticed Stanley's highly flushed face.

"Are you all right?" she asked him.

"Oh, yes, I am, Destini, for the most part, that is," he said. "Thank you for asking, though," he added, and then he paused a moment before continuing. "As a matter of fact, I have just received a bit of disturbing news from home is all. A local farming company, you see, had an option for a section of our land for outright purchase. Now, it seems, because of some pending litigation, which is moving along briskly to a possible class action suit against them, things have suddenly changed. They gave me their initial deposit, but, as per the parameters of the contract, they just reneged on their purchase agreement."

"Well, I do declare, Stanley," Dee Dee began, as she dropped her jaw and rolled her eyes in dramatic fashion. "What does that mean? You and Anna Mary have to stay at the Waldorf now, rather than the Pierre the next time you go to New York for theater and shopping? Oh, and, Stanley, honey, I know you're a

Yankee, but Destini and I have been at your table for several minutes now and we are perfectly parched. Where are your manners?"

"You know, Dee Dee, I have never particularly cared for you, but I will buy you a drink," Stanley curtly replied, and he motioned for the waiter.

"I know how you feel about me, sugar," Dee Dee said, smiling as if his words didn't offend her in the least. "Quite frankly, no one in the county has ever particularly cared for you, if you must know the truth. You have a superior education and bearing being from New England and all, but not so superior that you didn't live mostly on Anna Mary's money all these years."

Destini nonchalantly poked her in the ribs, but Dee Dee was on a roll and so she continued.

"Did you ever feel just a twinge of guilt when you ate off that silver that was paid for by all those old slave holders from years ago, Stanley?" Dee Dee rhetorically asked. "But, really, honey, neither Destini nor I are interested in what you like or don't like. Fortunately, we don't have to give a hoot. I just came over to ask about your granddaughter and inquire how she's getting along."

"She's doing just wonderful," Anna Mary interjected, never changing her expression from the pasted-on smile she always wore. "She's in the seventh grade now. It's so hard to believe. She is so beautiful, too. Let me show you a photo."

Destini and Dee Dee both admired the photo of

the child, and they oohed and ahhed over it for a good spcll, while Stanley sat and stewed.

"Anna Mary, I want to ask you and ol' hateful guts over there a question," Dee Dee began, in a tone of voice that was flat as a pancake.

At this, Stanley rolled his eyes and said, "Well, I have to admit, you've never talked behind our backs, Dee Dee."

"No, I never have and I never will," she said. "You see, I have more money than you, more land, more everything, and so I never feared you, Stanley. The worst you could have done to me is to have my lights turned off when you were head of the power company, but I'll shut up about that for the moment. My attention now turns from you, Stanley, over to your lovely wife," Dee Dee kept on, but then she hesitated for a second. "Oh, waiter! Bring us another round and put them on Mr. Williams' tab!" she added, loud enough for the entire room of diners to hear.

Destini could see the hairs on Stanley's neck spring to attention like little tin soldiers. Even though it truly embarrassed her, she was beginning to enjoy every minute of Dee Dee's outrageous, public display of distaste for the man sitting beside her.

It took no time at all for the waiter to bring them another round of drinks, and then Dee Dee continued her spiel. It was almost as if she had advance notice that Anna Mary and Stanley were going to be at the restaurant tonight, Destini thought.

"Anna Mary, I'm going to be married next year at

Camp EZ on Thanksgiving, and I want you to be in charge of directing my wedding," Dee Dee said, about to dish out compliments like a true Southern belle. "Nobody can organize more effectively than you. I have seen you in action many times and I was always truly impressed with the way you handled things. I would also like that beautiful angel grandchild of yours, Mary Selena, to be a junior bridesmaid in my wedding."

Anna Mary didn't say anything at first. She simply snatched the napkin from her lap and began to dab at her eyes. Then, she stood up from the table and went around to hug not only Dee Dee, but Destini, too.

"Of course, I would be honored, and, of course, Mary Selena will be a part of the wedding," the weeping woman said. "I can't wait to go back home to Seraph Springs and talk with all of you in about a month, if that's okay. I will call you beforehand and either come over to your house, or you can come to mine, and we'll discuss the details more."

Stanley rolled his eyes again and obviously didn't care who saw him, and then Dee Dee slyly winked at Destini.

"Stanley," she said, as sweet as mush. "I just know you and Anna Mary will want to host a welcome party for us a couple days ahead of time at the Jarrellson house. Perhaps, a champagne brunch?"

Stanley's eyes widened and he stiffened in his seat.

"For how many?" he asked, clearly stunned at the suggestion.

"Oh, not many," Dee Dee said. "A hundred,

maybe... maybe a few more. Oh, and Stanley, I want good champagne... some Moet White Star or Veuve Cliquot? None of that cheap fizz water, honey," she added.

Everyone laughed. Everyone except Stanley, that is.

"Mr. Stanley, you mentioned something about a lawsuit with a farming company and I think you may be referring to *Feed the World Organics*," Destini interrupted, changing the subject. "Do you know any more than that?" she asked him.

"No, not much, really," he said. "All I heard was there have been some iffy reports about groundwater quality lately, especially since that new farm corporation... and yes, you are correct... it is *Feed the World Organics*... in fact, they are the ones who reneged on my land deal. Anyway, I heard they were purchasing thousands of acres of old worn out land in Seraph Springs. From what I understand, they are owned by some foreign investors, one of whom is Dimitri Smith, I believe."

"Yes, Mr. Stanley. That's what I heard, too," Destini said. "I remember Mr. Hamp would call those places sand soaks, and I won't say what else he used to call 'em," she added, grinning as she shook her head.

"Well, I will," Dee Dee piped up. "Uncle Hamp used to say you'd have to stand on four sacks of fertilizer on that sandy land just to raise your temperature."

Everyone laughed at Dee Dee's comment, even Stanley this time.

"Anyway, Destini, because of the concerns voiced about the way that land is being handled, it seems the federal government has suddenly become more interested in what's actually going on there," Stanley explained.

"I see," Destini said, nodding her head. "They're probably just trying to cover their own you know what's, since they's the ones givin' out permits like there's no tomorrow."

"Could be," Stanley said. "Anyway, random water samples have been taken from residents' wells and alerts have been given to the local authorities, so they can warn people not to eat the fish from the river in certain areas. They also announced how many fish it would be safe to eat if caught in those areas of the river, as well as various creeks, where fertilizer and pesticide runoff may be entering the water. It just seems to keep snowballing into more and more of an issue."

"Well, that's concerning, since they claim to be all about organic farming," Destini said.

"Yes, it is," Stanley agreed.

"The way I heard it is that *Feed the World Organics* is owned by one of the nation's foremost technological giants and the LLC contains the names of people who have those generic names, but who probably have no idea what the company is about," Dee Dee interjected.

"I'm sure you're right about that," Stanley said. "However, the company sends those people a bonus check each year to keep them happy, satisfied and quiet. Once a year, they all go to the corporate headquarters down in Miami where they're put up at a luxury hotel. Then, they're wined and dined for a few days before they're asked to sign a sheath of papers that you know they don't even take the time to read. I heard they even authorized company officers to use a stamp signature or, believe it or not, offered to sign for them."

"Well, that don't sound right, now, does it?" Destini asked.

"No, it doesn't," Stanley said. "You're correct, too, about the company's claim that all their crops are grown organically. Do you know Dr. Candace Carlisle? You know... she taught biology and chemistry for years over at the community college in Marsdale."

"I believe she goes by the name Doc, of all things," Dee Dee said.

"Yes, I believe you're right, Dee Dee," Stanley said. "Anyway, her nephew, Clarence, lives in that little red, white and blue house not far from where you live, Destini."

"Yes, I remember both of them," Destini said.

Dee Dee laughed. "She was a strange bird, ol' Doc, but she was a good teacher. One of the best I ever had. Someone said her grandfather was some kind of big botany professor up north and that she inherited a lot of money. Clarence, bless his heart, had strabismus so terribly until Doc Carlisle finally sprang for surgery. It was horrible. You never knew if the kid was looking at you or the person standing next to you."

Anna Mary blushed and giggled, and said, "Dee Dee, you bad thing! It's the truth, though. Bless his heart. For all Doc Carlisle's uniqueness, she and Clarence never once missed attending church at Seraph Springs Methodist. Remember those mean Brandon boys who'd make Clarence cry, just to see if his tears would run down the back of his neck instead of down his cheeks?"

"Oh, my, yes!" Dee Dee exclaimed. "Both those boys are in jail now, though, serving time for repeated domestic violence incidents, from what I heard."

"Good," Anna Mary said. "That's where they should be. Anyway, Clarence has written so many nationally award winning books about the waterways of Florida that it's almost unbelievable," she went on. "He wrote most of it from home, except when his mother took a few trips with him to different places. I remember they always took that old hound dog of theirs with them... what did they call him?"

"Crap!" Dee Dee shouted, and then she giggled when everyone in the restaurant turned and stared at her.

"Have you ever heard of such a name for a dog?" Anna Mary gasped.

"Well, they found him near the entrance of Consolidated Regional Applied Phosphate... you know... C-R-A-P," Dee Dee said, still laughing. "I'm glad they finally changed their name to something simpler. Now, it's just Consolidated, right?"

"Last I heard," Anna Mary said.

"I recall those two picketed and screamed about that company for years, so it's understandable that they would name the dog Crap," Dee Dee explained, still chuckling. "Not a very charitable acronym for a company that pays over half the property taxes in Campbell County. You gotta admit, though, those two are definitely unique people."

"Oh, yes," Stanley said, joining in the conversation. "Supposedly, the two of them have had threats of all kinds made to them. That old rusted van of theirs, I remember, was egged by a couple of workers from the phosphate company, but it didn't deter them. They just kept on."

"At least they were consistent in what they pursued," Dee Dee said.

"Anyway, being who they are and what they're about, they shared with Anna Mary and me... and don't ask me why we were elected to become their confidante..." Stanley continued.

"I can answer that question," Anna Mary butted in, interrupting her husband. "Remember when Candace first moved here, and then her husband was killed shortly afterward while working at the phosphate plant? Well, I became her friend around that time, and I still consider her a friend and confidante. I don't care how strange she seems to other people."

"Good for you, Anna Mary," Dee Dee said. "You are so right. Everybody needs someone, and it doesn't matter what's on the outside, honey. The heart is what counts. It sounds like you made a wise decision."

"Thank you, my dear," Anna Mary said. "Despite what some people may think, there's a bit more to me than just moonlight and magnolias."

"I never had a doubt about that," Dee Dee said, smiling at her. "I remember who tutored me and got me through college English and composition. Don't think I've forgotten. Oh, and remember those godawful cotillion things we had to attend when they sent us off to finishing camp in Charleston? If you hadn't come with me and stayed with me in that apartment Aunt Hattie rented, I never would have made it through that summer."

"Ladies, may I move on with the story?" Stanley said, interrupting the two women's walk down memory lane.

"Of course, Stanley," Anna Mary said. "Please do go on."

"Well, Doc Carlisle and her nephew found an open gap in the fence out there at *Feed the World Organics* and they crawled through. They had a high-tech zoom camera, as well as a video camera with them. What they captured on film is fairly damning for the company."

"Wow! Really?" Destini asked.

"Yes, really," Stanley said. "First of all, those crops they're growing are about as organic as that plaster column on the wall over there," he said, pointing across the room. "They're using pesticides and insecticides out the ying-yang, and I mean gallons and gallons of it."

"Oh, dear," Anna Mary said.

"The fertilizer they're using is being purchased

directly from the local phosphate company, too, but that's the only link the company has to them. The phosphate company isn't dumb, you know. With the amount of fertilizer being purchased by *Feed the World Organics*, they are simply doing business. Of course, they're not saying much, and they may not even know what's going on because *Feed the World Organics* has numerous other agricultural operations throughout the country and the world that aren't organic farms."

"This is getting interesting," Destini said.

"Secondly, *Feed the World Organics* is part of a huge organization that owns hundreds of companies, large and small," Stanley continued. "Including one of the largest agricultural/chemical companies in the world that produces massive amounts of insecticides, pesticides and herbicides. That company is located in some remote part of North Dakota, but it ships and sends its products all over the world."

"Wow, I agree with you, Destini," Dee Dee said. "This is truly getting more and more interesting. Please go on, Stanley."

"Well, Doc and Clarence, after they crawled through that fence, saw hundreds of migrant workers wearing masks and gloves and white suits, and they were throwing that powdered poison out by hand on a lot of those crops they're growing," Stanley said. "Then, they saw others on tractors, who were spraying insecticides and pesticides on all the plants. They also found about a three hundred acre field of flue cured tobacco being grown by the company, even though they claim that all they grow are crops to feed the world."

"Hmmm…" Dee Dee said, scrunching up her face. "Maybe they're making chewing tobacco and putting it in packets that say, "Chew and Swallow" in a hundred different languages. Then, they send it around the globe, and in reality it's de-worming little children."

"Anything is possible these days," Destini said. "I wouldn't put it past anyone to do that."

"Let me tell you about something else they found, and this is the part that really concerns me," Stanley continued. "Not only are tons of those poisons going into the ground, but in those warehouses, evidently, they're bringing in some chemicals that are, shall we say, a bit out of date. Then, during the night, they dump those chemicals onto two huge fields at the back of their property. Through those fields runs Wilson Creek and its tributary Baby Branch, and these run right into…" he trailed off, raising his eyebrows.

"Lord have mercy!" Destini gasped. "They run right into the Suwannee River itself. Right there where Mama Tee used to go fishin'… right there where Wilson Creek runs into the river. Mr. Hamp's old cabin isn't far from it. Now that I think about it, Mama Tee told me on two or three different occasions when she came back from fishin' that something near the creek wasn't smellin' just right. Essie and Duke said the same thing. I told her she was crazy, but she fired back at me. "Say what you want, but it ain't no sweet shrub or no honeysuckle or huckleberry blooms, and it ain't river mud, neither," she told me. She said she knew all the smells of nature and the river, and what she was smellin' was different, like cleaning fluid mixed with bleach."

"Oh, wow," Dee Dee said. "That's not good."

"No, it ain't," Destini said. "Mama Tee said she didn't smell it all the time, but most of the time she was there fishin'."

"Looks like Doc and Clarence are tellin' the truth, huh?" Dee Dee asked.

"Yep, then one day Mama Tee, Duke and Essie went there to fish and Duke said he seen soft shelled turtles... we call 'em cooters... not one or two, but a bunch of 'em lying dead on the river bank. Mama Tee said she thought it was strange, but Duke said he also saw a bunch of alligators around 'em, so he figured the gators had gotten to 'em. A few days later, though, he seen buzzards circling around the area, so he went and checked it out. He came back later and said he seen quite a few dead gators on the bank of the river where them cooters had been. He said them gators weren't killed with no shotgun, either."

"Is that when they stopped fishing there?" Dee Dee asked her.

"Yep," she said. "They decided to just fish in the lakes up near Camp EZ."

"Smart move," Stanley said.

"There is definitely something fishy going on at *Feed the World Organics*," Dee Dee said.

"They're hiding something, for sure," Destini

agreed. "Well, it sounds like a bunch of business for whomever Phil Jr. is representing," she added. "You remember my baby, Phil Brainard, Jr., right?" she asked, and Stanley nodded. "Well, he's involved in this case. Anyway, thank you for telling me about the lawsuit, Mr. Stanley. It seems you knew a lot more than you thought you did. It was good to see you and Miss Anna Mary."

"Yes, it sure was good to see y'all," Dee Dee butted in, with a huge, fake smile plastered on her face, just like Anna Mary's.

"We best be gettin' back to our table and let these folks enjoy their dinner," Destini said, nudging Dee Dee in the ribs, as she stood up from the table.

Dee Dee, however, didn't seem ready to leave yet. So, Destini literally had to pry her from her chair by the arm. Dee Dee, being the brash Dee Dee that she was, had to get in one last zing before leaving their table.

"Well, I am so pleased, Stanley, that you got the chance to see me one more time, honey," she said to him. "I know my beauty has always dazzled you. You just couldn't get enough of my Southern beauty, could you? Anna Mary, always good seeing you, honey."

"Take care, Dee Dee. I'll be in touch," Anna Mary said. "Oh, Dee Dee, I almost forgot to ask. Are you wearing the Jarrellson veil on your wedding day?"

"I sure am, sugar. You know, Aunt Hattie said her mama told her that in Brussels, Belgium several of the nuns in that convent went blind making that lace."

"That's true," Anna Mary said, nodding in

agreement.

"That lace is truly priceless," Dee Dee said. "None was made after the end of the nineteen-thirties. That veil was purchased when my father's great-great grandfather was going to be married. It was the first wedding in the Seraph Springs United Methodist Church, which was built out of Jarrellson timber, by the way. The veil first pranced down the aisle on the head of a Jarrellson bride in the fall of 1840," she added, as if she was speaking from a podium to a crowded room.

"I have the veil at my house here, Dee Dee," Anna Mary said. "Come by tomorrow. You know where I live. I will expect you around four in the afternoon. You and Destini and Miss Sissy come by. I'll serve tea and by that time Mary Selena will be home. You'll have a chance to visit with her."

Destini, whose countenance had brightened at the invitation, closed her eyes for a few seconds.

"Thank you, Jesus," she silently prayed. "Thank you for allowing me to see this child again. Oh, and thank you, Dee Dee. You're somethin' else, girl."

"Stanley, Anna Mary, it was good talking with you both, and we will be visiting with you soon," Dee Dee said. "Truly, this was a good talk. I want you both to know, and I mean this sincerely… I have often prayed for you. I don't know the pain of losing a child, but I do know that your son was, without a doubt, one of the kindest young men ever."

"Amen to that," Destini said. "He was always my baby, and he never forgot me. I will never forget him, either. He's always right here," she added, as she placed her hand over her heart.

"Thank you both for that," Anna Mary said, as her eyes welled with tears.

Both she and Stanley stood up and embraced the two women. It was something Destini had never seen Stanley Williams do since she had known him.

"He did love you, Destini, and we did not treat you fairly," Stanley told her. "I pray you can forgive us. I relive my child's life each day, and I thank God we have little Mary Selena. I don't know what..." he trailed off, as his voice choked and his eyes filled with tears.

"Don't think about that, Mr. Stanley," Destini said. "I do forgive you with my whole heart. It was not you. It was the way you was raised. In your heart you thought you were doing right. You can't give what you don't have. You're a changed man, but that child's death didn't change you. I know who did, and it was Jesus."

"You are absolutely right," he said.

Meanwhile, Anna Mary and Dee Dee held each other and wept. It was obvious they didn't care what others in the restaurant were thinking as they stared at the two women. They were in a world unto themselves and it was a world of compassion, understanding, and what Destini had always said was so important... love... unconditional love.

By the time Destini and Dee Dee returned to their table, Miss Sissy and Justin, it seemed, had given up on them and decided to hang out at the bar and throw back a few cold ones. Surprisingly, or not, Dee Dee's and Destini's desserts were sitting on the table untouched and waiting on them.

Chapter 13

She didn't know why, but for days now Destini had been having a strange, nagging feeling deep inside her soul. It was the same kind of emptiness she felt right before Jerri Faye Linton's passing. The beloved Jerri Faye was born with Down's syndrome and when she died in her mid-twenties, the entire town of Seraph Springs came out to her funeral to pay their respects, as she had been loved by everyone. It was a big deal and a huge shock to everyone. It was probably one of the most beautiful funerals ever held in the town, though.

Destini also had the same nagging feeling not too long before she lost Hamp Brayerford, so she was rightfully concerned that something dreadful was about to happen. On the way back to Miss Sissy's house after their delightful dinner and the surprise visit with Anna Mary and Stanley, she started humming a song. Dee Dee asked her to sing it instead of just humming it.

"It's one of my favorite, old African American gospel songs and you sing it so beautifully," Dee Dee said, encouraging her. And so, she did.

"There's a storm out over the ocean and it's moving this-a-way.
If your soul's not anchored in Jesus, you will surely drift away."

After she finished that song, she immediately went into another.

> *"Oh, oh, I know I've been changed.*
> *Oh, oh, I know I've been changed.*
> *Oh, oh, I know I've been changed.*
> *The angels in heaven done signed my name."*

Later that night, Destini had another remarkable dream. In her dream she saw two deer – a large doe and a baby fawn – wander down to the water's edge of the Suwannee River to drink. Then, she watched them suddenly fall over and neither one of them had a mark on them; no bullet wounds, no arrows, no nothing. They just fell over.

Right after that, she spotted two wild ducks at her feet. She didn't know from where they came, but she reached down to pick up one of them. When she did, however, both ducks vanished into the mist. They just disappeared.

She had always set great store by dreams that were out of the ordinary. When she'd awaken from such dreams, she'd be in a cold sweat, like she was now. Normally, she wouldn't have resorted to this, but she shook Dee Dee awake and told her about the dream.

"When we get home, I want you to go to Mama Tee and you tell her about these dreams you've been having lately," Dee Dee told her. "I'll guess, more than likely, she'll be able to tell you what it all means."

"I'll sure do that, Dee Dee. I sure will."

"Well, now that we're both wide awake, let's go down to the kitchen and scrape up some grub. I'm hungry again," Dee Dee suggested.

So, the two girls went into Miss Sissy's kitchen and rooted around for something to eat. Miss Sissy evidently heard all the racket they were making and she stormed into the kitchen with a ball bat in her hand.

"What the heck?!" she shouted, when she saw two silhouettes moving back and forth in the dim light of the refrigerator. "What are you doin' in my kitchen?!"

"Whoa, Miss Sissy! Don't hit us! We're just hungry!" Dee Dee shouted back at her.

"Oh, my goodness!" Miss Sissy yelled, as she grabbed her chest and let out a huge sigh of relief. "I thought there was a burglar in the house!"

"I'm sorry," Dee Dee said. "I'm so sorry."

"Boy, you two really had me going there for a minute," Miss Sissy said, managing to laugh about it now.

"Aw, come on, Miss Sissy," Destini said, laughing. "Do you really think a burglar would break in just to eat somethin' from your fridge?"

"Hey, you never know nowadays. I keep a lot of good darned food in there," Miss Sissy retorted. "Look, why don't you two kitchen bandits join me in the den? There's a wonderful, old classic film on the television right now."

"Can we get something to eat first?" Dee Dee asked.

"Yeah, sure, whatever you want," Miss Sissy said,

shaking her head. "How about some popcorn and hot cocoa?" she suggested.

"Works for me," Dee Dee said.

"Good. When y'all get done making it, bring it into the den," Miss Sissy said, and she turned and left the room.

"Do you believe that woman?" Dee Dee asked Destini.

"Oh, yeah, I believe her, all right," she said, and the two girls had a good laugh, as they prepared the snacks.

About fifteen minutes later, the three friends were curled up on the couch watching the movie, while reminiscing some more about the good old days during all the commercials. It was close to two o'clock when they finally called it quits and went to bed.

Chapter 14

At about nine o'clock the next morning, Destini and Dee Dee were in the kitchen finishing up breakfast, while Miss Sissy, who had gotten up at the crack of dawn, was in the shower.

"Ummm, Destini, honey, isn't this egg dish just melt-in-your-mouth delicious?" Dee Dee asked.

"It sure is," Destini said. "Miss Sissy is a pretty good cook, huh?"

"Honey, I do believe this was Justin's doin's, not Miss Sissy's," Dee Dee corrected her. "By the way, where is that handsome young man?"

"I think I saw him out front watering Miss Sissy's flowers."

"What a guy, eh?" Dee Dee asked, laughing. "Well, sweetie, you sit there and drink your coffee. I'll take care of these dishes," she added, and then she took their plates and silverware over to the sink.

"Thanks," Destini said, and then her mind wandered off to a place deep within her heart from days gone by.

She had known Dee Dee and her cousin, Carl Alvin Campbell, most all of her life. They played together as children and socialized together at Camp EZ as adults. Plus, Mama Tee had raised half the

Campbell family with her own children and grandchildren. She even partially raised Dee Dee.

Destini recalled how, on numerous occasions, Dee Dee would get into an argument with her Aunt Hattie and then steal the keys to her old, red Buick. She used to brag about the amount of dust she left boiling on the white sand road behind her as she sped away. When Destini would see her coming up the road to Mama Tee's, she'd always shout, "Here she comes!"

Mama Tee would just sit there and smile like the patient woman she always was. Then, she'd say to Destini, "Go slice that girl some sweet potato pie and bring a glass of that cold milk out here. Then, make yourself scarce for 'bout a half hour. I know someone who needs some motherin' right now."

Destini would reluctantly abide by her grandmother's wishes, of course. In the end she could tell from the way Dee Dee would walk up to the house that she really was upset about something and needed Mama Tee's maternal advice.

Dee Dee and Carl Alvin were two of the most well-to-do white children of their generation in the area, and even more so now, since their Uncle Hamp died and left them a sizable inheritance. They were born to privilege and power, yet, when they were younger, they made their way out to Mama Tee's quaint, vine-covered house in the woods all the time. Dee Dee would say later that it was so peaceful there with all the lush Formosa trees surrounding the house that she never wanted to leave. Their many visits often included spending the night and eating meals with Mama Tee's family.

You could find them at Mama Tee's every Saturday afternoon, too, and always on the old woman's birthday, as well as at Easter and most of the other major holidays when they were in town.

Mama Tee referred to them as "my babies". Both of them, many times, had nestled up against Mama Tee's ample and loving bosom, pouring out their hearts to her as they cried over this, that or the other. She listened, she comforted and she never failed to offer sage advice. Hamp Brayerford once said Mama Tee was the "Citizen of the Century" for Campbell County.

"Well, enough of that," Destini thought, shaking off all those old memories for the moment. "I suppose I should call home and make sure everything is okay. I ain't talked with no one since me and Dee Dee left Jacksonville."

With that, she picked up her cell phone from the table and punched in a familiar number. She was duly taken by surprise when Carl Alvin answered the telephone at Camp EZ.

"Why, Carl Alvin, you are out and about early this mornin'," she said, knowing that he normally never got into gear before noon. "Where's Nadine and Wanda Faye? What's goin' on?"

"Oh, the girls are here somewhere. Don't worry," he said. "As for me, I had to come out and take care of a little business," he said, matter-of-factly.

Destini heard something rather strange in his voice

that she couldn't quite put her finger on. Not to be deterred, she delved deeper.

"Something's not right, Carl Alvin," she said to him. "I can hear it your voice. What's goin' on?" she asked again.

Dee Dee, who had just sat back down beside Destini at the kitchen table, had been listening to the one-sided conversation and obviously couldn't stand it any longer.

"Hand me that dang phone," she ordered Destini, and then she hit the speakerphone button and laid the phone on the table between them. "Carl Alvin, you cut the crap right now!" she yelled. "What the hell is going on there?"

"Oh... hi, Dee Dee, uhh... I... I, uhh... I didn't want to worry you and Destini, but... but Essie is not well," he stammered. "She is really *not* well," he emphasized. "She's been complaining of stomach cramps for days. Last night it got so bad that Duke had to take her to the hospital in Gainesville. She has a low grade fever and she's puking up everything she eats. She's dehydrated, too. Right now, the doctors are trying to get the fever down and they're doing a bunch of tests on her."

"Oh, Lord have mercy," Destini mumbled, as her eyes grew wide in fear.

"Then, yesterday morning, Miss Jewell didn't show up for church," Carl Alvin continued.

"What did you say?!" Dee Dee gasped. "Miss Jewell missed church?! She never misses church! Ever!"

"I know, I know," Carl Alvin said. "When the girls got to her house, they found her in a similar condition as Essie. I don't know what is happening around here, Dee Dee, but it has us all more than concerned."

"Listen up, Carl Alvin," Dee Dee began. "First, get a hold of yourself. You gotta be the strong one here, okay? Me and Destini have to go to Anna Mary's this afternoon. Meanwhile, we'll get everything packed up now before we go, so we can make a quick exit over to the airport. I want you to arrange for that charter plane to be here in New Orleans by six o'clock this evening. Do you understand?" she asked him, although, she didn't wait for him to respond. "We're coming home, Carl Alvin. We may not be able to do anything once we get there, but we're coming home. By the way, how is everyone else holding up?"

"Everyone's pretty upset, as you might imagine," he replied. "The girls, Nadine and Wanda Faye, are going crazy, and Mama Tee, Bunnye... well, everyone has been better. They need you right now, Dee Dee. Be thinking on the way home how you can take their minds off all this business, and pray, honey. Do pray. Meanwhile, I will make all the arrangements."

"Thanks, Carl Alvin," Dee Dee said, and they both hung up.

Destini was already crying, and then Miss Sissy entered the room. Dee Dee pulled her aside and explained what had happened.

"Something's not right," Dee Dee told her. "We love you, Miss Sissy, but we have to get home today."

"I completely understand, honey," Miss Sissy said. "Well, let me see…," she continued, scratching her head for a moment. "There are four things I can do for both of you. I can hug you, I can do your hair, I can pack your clothes, and I can call the sheriff and have him meet you at the airport in Jacksonville with an escort from the High Sheriff himself," she added with a wink. "That will whir you back to Seraph Springs in fast order."

"Ohh, thank you, Miss Sissy," Dee Dee said, and the two women hugged. "What would we do without you?"

Chapter 15

After Destini and Dee Dee got their bags packed, and after Miss Sissy styled their hair and attended to returning a few phone calls from her salon customers, Justin took all three women to the atelier shop of Madame Hortense. It would be their final words with her for a while.

After Madame Hortense's, they went to a couple of antique stores where some items were purchased for Carl Alvin, Miss Hattie and Miss Nanny. Destini also selected a gold necklace with a heart-shaped locket for Mary Selena and Dee Dee decided on a beautiful antique evening bag and fan for Anna Mary. She even broke down and bought a first edition copy of a major, best-selling book about engineering accomplishments in the Deep South for Stanley.

"I can't believe I'm buying something for this man," she muttered.

"You're a good person, Dee Dee," Destini told her. "That's why."

At four o'clock on the nose, they arrived at the magnificent, stately home of Anna Mary and Stanley Williams. Miss Sissy had some errands to attend to and said she and Justin would be back in one hour to pick them up and take them to the airport.

A quaint Creole cottage, as Anna Mary had described her New Orleans home before she left Seraph Springs, it definitely was not. A uniformed maid answered the door when Dee Dee knocked, and then she announced their arrival before escorting the two women into a spacious solarium.

"Please have a seat," she instructed them.

Moments later, a different maid rolled in an antique cart with a sterling silver tea service that held a large pitcher of lemonade, a pot of tea, half a dozen crystal glasses and several teacups. Slices of pound cake and small tea sandwiches had already been placed on the sideboard.

Anna Mary emerged about two minutes later from the hallway in a smart hunter green dress, simply cut, and wearing the heirloom Jarrellson pearls... three strands of them. Her hair was pulled back from her forehead into a bun, and her makeup, as always, was expertly done.

"Ladies, it's so good to see you again," she said. "I'm sorry, but Stanley won't be joining us. He had some business to take care of in town."

"That's quite all right," Destini told her. "Besides, I doubt he'd be much interested in talking about wedding veils."

"You're right about that," Anna Mary concurred.

"Miss Sissy sends her regards, as well," Dee Dee told her. "She had some errands to run."

"Tell her I missed seeing her," Anna Mary said.

After Dee Dee complimented her on how lovely

she looked, Anna Mary produced the Jarrellson veil from a beautifully jeweled box she was carrying.

Shortly thereafter, Mary Selena entered the solarium and her beauty took Destini's breath away. The child didn't hesitate for even a second before rushing full on into Destini's arms and hugging her tightly.

"Oh, honey, aren't you just a beautiful sight for these tired old eyes of mine," Destini said. "You are so pretty, and it is so good to see you."

"It's good to see you, too, Miss Destini," Mary Selena replied.

The child was dressed in a simple, deep cranberry-colored, velvet jumper and a beige colored blouse with big puffed sleeves. At her ears were a pair of pearl studs that had been given to her mother on her wedding day by the Jarrellsons and then passed down to her.

"Mary Selena, why don't you pour for us today, darling?" Anna Mary suggested. "You know how to do it, and then we will chat about Dee Dee's upcoming wedding. You know, the one in which you, my darling, are going to serve as an attendant."

Quietly, and with the ease of one who was much older, young Mary Selena presided over the afternoon tea with ease.

Dee Dee later told Destini that she couldn't help but notice the beauty of the child's skin, as well as the distinctive, graceful way she moved. She said she could see in her face the mixture of the Jarrellson features and the child's grandfather, whom Dee Dee said she had once seen at a polo match in Palm Beach. Even in advanced years, she said he was an extremely handsome man, and carried himself with dignity and authority.

After Mary Selena served everyone, Dee Dee reached into her designer shopping bag and retrieved the two gifts she bought for Anna Mary and Stanley.

"Oh, my word, Dee Dee," Anna Mary said, blushing. "You didn't have to bring us gifts. I'm so sorry, but I don't have any for you or Destini," she added, but she accepted the gifts just the same and placed them on the table beside her.

"We're just fine, Anna Mary," Destini interrupted. "Just being able to see Mary Selena is gift enough for me."

"Same here," Dee Dee said.

Moments later, when Destini presented Mary Selena with her gift, the little girl seemed overjoyed, as well as a little shocked at first. However, she immediately composed herself and expressed her appreciation to Destini with the grace of one born into royalty.

After about an hour's chit-chat about the veil, the upcoming wedding, and the preparations for it, it was time for Destini and Dee Dee to depart when they heard Miss Sissy and Justin pull up out front.

"Before you go, Miss Destini, could you tell me one story about my mama and daddy?" Mary Selena asked her.

"Why, yes, I can," Destini said, and before Anna

Mary could protest, Destini held up her hand with her palm facing toward her, signaling that she stay quiet.

"I remember like it was yesterday the first time I laid eyes on your mama," Destini began. "She was dressed in a beautiful white lace dress, and when she came down the stairs at your grandma and grandpa's house, the whole room went quiet. It made your daddy really turn around and take notice of her. I think it was love at first sight, too."

Mary Selena's eyes lit up and she went over to sit on Destini's lap.

"On their weddin' day, I never saw a more beautiful bride," Destini continued, smoothing the child's hair away from her face. "In fact, your mama was more than beautiful. She was other-worldly. She didn't just walk down that aisle at the Methodist church that very special day in Seraph Springs. She glided like a floating butterfly down that flower-petaled aisle. She looked just like the Queen of England."

Anna Mary and Dee Dee were both dabbing their faces with their handkerchiefs, as they watched the excitement on Mary Selena's face.

"Yes, ma'am," Destini went on. "See that gal over there? Miss Dee Dee? Well, she goin' have you lookin' just as beautiful on her weddin' day, which will be comin' up real soon. You can count on it, but before that weddin', you goin' come stay with me at Camp EZ for a bit. I have a little girl 'bout your age and I know the two of you will have a wonderful time together."

"That sounds so nice," Anna Mary said, breaking

up their little chat, as she stood up from her chair. "Thank you both for the visit," she said, almost as if she was anxious for them to leave. "Dee Dee, I will be talking to you soon about your wedding plans. I have already drawn some sketches of what I think the wedding area should look like and how the tables should be arranged. I'm keeping in mind the time of year, as well as the grounds at Camp EZ. I hope when I finish, you'll like what I have done."

"Anna Mary, I know clothes, Destini knows food and the camp, but you know the A to Z of entertaining in north Florida," Dee Dee said, standing up herself now. "Nobody can take that away from you, and you do it with such ease. At least it looks like ease to me. That's the reason I turned the wedding over to you."

"Well, I certainly do appreciate your trust in me," Anna Mary said, and she gave Dee Dee a hug.

"Well, we have to go now," Dee Dee said. "We're headed for the airport. I know our luggage has already been sent over by Miss Sissy. It was good to see you, Mary Selena. Come give me and Destini another hug."

The child hugged both of them and thanked them again for her necklace, which she was already wearing. Then, she presented both of them with a framed photograph of herself.

It was all Destini could do to keep herself together. She felt so blessed just being able to visit the child and see how beautiful and happy she was. As she and Dee Dee were leaving, Destini said a silent prayer to God, thanking him again for answering her prayers.

Chapter 16

On the way to the airport, Dee Dee, Destini and Miss Sissy talked about their visit, about the beauty of Mary Selena, about Justin and his exquisite physique, and about Miss Sissy's gracious hospitality, for which they both kept thanking her profusely.

By the time they arrived at the airport terminal and boarded the plane, Destini and Dee Dee had talked about all kinds of things, except what was most pressing on their minds. Right before the plane took off, Destini's cell phone rang. She couldn't believe her ears. It was Mama Tee, who never phoned anyone, ever.

"Guess who this is and who dialed this number?" Mama Tee yelled into the mouthpiece even before Destini could answer with a hello. "One of my babies, Phil, is here! Came and brought me breakfast. Yesterday, he went with me to the church service at Mt. Nebo! Lots o' peoples at the service, 'cludin' some mens from da gov'ment talkin' 'bout testin' our wells in dis part o' da county, and wantin' to test some o' the fish in the pond! You there, Destini?" she asked, taking a breath.

"I'm here, Mama Tee," Destini assured her.

"Good," she said. "You know that pond that's fed

by the little creek dat runs through the place? Well, my baby says we ought to do it, so dat's good enough for me!"

"Mama Tee, you don't have to yell," Destini told her, and she put the phone on speaker, so that Dee Dee could join in the conversation. "I can hear you just fine."

"Hey, Mama Tee," Dee Dee said, but the old woman ignored her.

"Now, let me talk to that baby," Destini said. "Remember, Mama Tee, he was my baby first."

Young Phil Brainard had grown up to become a fine young man, and one that Destini was so proud of. He had a wife and child now, but he had never been a stranger throughout the years. He always kept in touch one way or another.

"I don't care whose baby he was first!" Mama Tee continued shouting, as Destini cringed and partially covered her ears, while Dee Dee sat there giggling to herself. "He mine always! You see who he spent the day wif! And I got somethin' else I'm goin' tell you, so don't get yer dander up! I decided and done told Duke to deed this boy a couple o' acres o' land across the road here, just down from him and Essie! He wants to build a cabin on it! He offered me lots o' money! I told him to give the money to Mt. Nebo and that's what he done! It goin' help buy us a new church van!"

"Well, I don't think you shoulda give it to him," Destini joked, which was evidently the wrong thing to do at the moment, because Mama Tee immediately fired back.

"I don't give a damn what you does and don't like, missy!" she yelled even louder. "I'll slap you into next Sunday if you sass me! You can tell Queenie there wid you de same! Pinned some of the first diapers on her lil' behind, and I can still tear it up! I'm a grown woman! I do what da hell I want wid what's mine!"

Dee Dee was doubled over, holding her hand over her mouth, she was laughing so hard.

"You go on, Mama Tee, and do what you want," Dee Dee managed to say a few seconds later. "I love you, and we're bringing you something pretty for Christmas. Destini almost forgot about you, but I reminded her."

Destini gasped, and then she playfully smacked Dee Dee's arm. "Don't egg her on," she whispered to her.

"Well, it be good somebody remembers!" Mama Tee shouted. "I can tell bof y'all, it'll be hell to pay wid no Christmas giff for me! Since y'all can both hear me, it seems, lil' Phil wanna say somethin', too. Go 'head, baby, tell dese bad girls what on yer mind."

"Destini, Dee Dee, this is Phil," he said in a normal tone of voice.

"Well, we knows that, young man," Destini teased him.

"Hang on a sec. Let me put you on speaker," he said. "Okay, now Mama Tee can hear you, as well."

"Phil, what's going on?" Dee Dee asked. "Can we help you some way, sugar?"

"I hope so, Dee Dee," he said. "What I'm going to tell you and Destini is kind of… well, undercover at the moment. I want you to remember that, okay?"

"We understand," Dee Dee assured him.

"During the past few weeks, I tested several wells within a five-mile radius of Mama Tee's farm," he began. "Without exception, they all show fairly significant signs of contamination. I can't say for certain that it's caused from that farming operation, but I'm bringing in some more experts from my department, who are coming down on their own dime to look into this."

"What kind of contamination?" Destini asked.

"Mercury, lead, arsenic, and a host of other toxins," he explained. "Levels are higher… much higher than what they should be," he added.

"Could this cause sickness over a period of time?" Destini wanted to know.

"If you're asking if this could have caused Essie's and Miss Jewell's trouble, the answer is yes, it could have. They have both drank and bathed in that water for a long time. What they're experiencing right now could be related. I have a friend who's a medical doctor. He's coming down here, too, so I need to find a place for all of them to stay. I'm looking into that now."

"Well, honey, look no further," Dee Dee said. "They are all now guests at Camp EZ, compliments of one of the owners."

"Dee Dee, you know we're booked through the

New Year," Destini quietly protested.

"I don't care if we are," Dee Dee said. "Call them all and tell them something has come up, except the Fernandez family, that is. My fiance's family can stay with Aunt Hattie in town. She doesn't have anyone else in that big, old mausoleum, anyway."

"Okay, then," Destini said. "I believe the rest of them could be put up comfortably at Mr. Hamp's cabin on the river, now that Duke and Essie have added on to it, and they can stay in my room and Bunnye's room at the camp. We'll just move in with one of the girls, Nadine or Wanda Faye, until this is through."

"Do you mean it?" Phil asked.

"Yes, of course, we mean it," Destini said. "Now, you tell those scientist boys they goin' have to help some with Christmas decoratin' and that kinda thing at Camp EZ 'cause we always get an early start, but they'll be fine. We know how to get 'em movin'. They'll be welcomed with open arms. How many will there be, includin' yourself?"

"There will be eight of us, including my wife and daughter," Phil said.

"Well, shoot, if that's all, then we still got room for four more, even if me and Bunnye stay there," Destini said. "Dee Dee, looks like the Fernandez family can stay at the camp after all, provided they don't mind the company of the scientists."

"Oh, that's great," Dee Dee said. "I'm sure they won't mind... if the men Phil is bringing can keep Ricardo's dad from talking them to death, that is. Oh, that man loves to talk, and so does his wife."

"I have a remedy for that," Destini piped up. "I'll bring Mama Tee over, as well as Sister Violet Jackson, the chairman of our Stewardess Board out at Mt. Nebo. If between them they can't keep Señor and Señora Fernandez out-talked, then, honey, there's not a cow in the state of Florida and it's a heiferless range."

"Perfect," Dee Dee said, laughing at Destini's witticism. "Phil, get those scientist boys in, honey. Are any of them single men? Destini is an unmarried woman, you know."

"Ooohh, Dee Dee, you so bad!" Destini said, this time slapping her arm hard enough to leave a mark.

"Ouch, girl!" Dee Dee said. "Pay her no mind, Phil."

"As a matter of fact, Destini, one of the men, Dr. Douglas is newly widowed," Phil offered. "He spent his life in research, and he's a nice man… quiet, but still "done in" a bit by his wife, Earnestine's, death."

"Bless his heart," Destini said. "Well, Phil, I ain't shopping for no husband right now. You know that, nor no boyfriend, either. I do hope you can find out what the trouble is at home, though. That's what I'm interested in. I do want to see what the deal is with the water and what's wrong with Essie and Miss Jewell."

"We all do," Phil said. "I've had concerns for some time. Remember when I was a little boy, and you would talk to me here at Mama Tee's on spring afternoons and during the summer, and we'd fish in that creek and that little spring-fed pond?"

"Yes, I remember," Destini said. "I remember how Mama Tee kept special clothes and shoes for you to go into that creek 'cause Miss Julie always put up such a fuss when you came home all wet and sandy. You spent so much time in that creek and playing on the bank, but you always had time to come up to the house for a piece of Miss Jewell's chocolate swirl cake."

At this, Destini choked up and the tears began rolling down her cheeks.

"Poor Miss Jewell, poor Essie," Destini cried. "Lawd, here I been in New Orleans havin' a grand ol' time and them two sick. I need to get home. I *really* need to get home."

"Dee Dee!" Mama Tee shouted into the phone. "I'm dependin' on you to get our girl there calmed down and feelin' better. Sister Violet is here now and we goin' sing a song to calm my little Destini. Is you listenin', Destini?"

"I'm listenin', Mama Tee."

At that, the two ladies began singing.

"Nobody but you, Lord, nobody but you,
Nobody but you, Lord, nobody but you,
When I was in trouble you brought me over.
Nobody but you, Lord, nobody but you.

He's a mighty good doctor, nobody but you,
He's a mighty good doctor, nobody but you.
When I was in trouble you brought me over.
Nobody but you, Lord, nobody but you.

He's a mighty good lawyer, nobody but you.
He's a mighty good lawyer, nobody but you.
When I was in trouble you brought me over.
Nobody but you, Lord, nobody but you."

"Do you feel more encouraged now, Destini?" Mama Tee asked when they finished singing.

"Yes, ma'am, I do," Destini said. "Mama Tee, Sister Violet, let the folks at home know that after we land in Jacksonville, I do plan on comin' home as soon as I can. We'll be gettin' in late tonight. First thing tomorrow mornin', after I visit with my baby for a bit, I'm goin' to the hospital in Gainesville. Phil, if you're listenin', I want you to come with me. Will you come with me?"

Destini heard him take in his breath and his voice caught in his throat, the way it did when he was a little boy.

"Now, Destini, you know I would do anything for you. Go anywhere. My God, you've never asked me to do a thing for you. Of course, I will. I'll be glad to go with you, drive you, whatever you need."

"You can drive us all," Dee Dee interjected. "We will all be going. Me, Destini, Nadine, Wanda Faye and Carl Alvin. We're all going. You can drive us all."

"Now, Dee Dee, how you know we all goin' be goin'?" Destini asked.

"As I said, Phil, we will all be going," Dee Dee said again, ignoring Destini's question. "We can take Carl

Alvin's big SUV. It has enough room for all of us. If it doesn't, I'll order a limo. We're all going… period."

"That won't be necessary," Phil said. "I have a van that's about as big as a bus. We can ride down there in it, okay?"

"Works for me," Dee Dee said.

Destini didn't question any further and she could hear Mama Tee chuckling in the background.

"You hear Queenie has spoken," Mama Tee said. "You get 'em in line, Queenie. I 'spect them folk in Gainesville won't know what hit 'em when all of us step out of that big ol' van in our glory with Phil," Mama Tee went on. "Destini, I'll be there at the camp early tomorrow mornin'. You have breakfast ready. Sister Violet will bring me. We be there around seven and after we eat we'll head down to the hospital. Love you chil'. See you then."

Before hanging up, Destini heard Mama Tee and Sister Violet break into a song again and then the phone went dead.

Chapter 17

The private charter jet began its taxi out to the runway for takeoff from New Orleans. Once the plane was airborne and leveled out, Destini reached over and took hold of Dee Dee's hand, her lifetime friend. It was the same hand she had reached for so often over the years, in times of happiness, as well as sadness. Dee Dee squeezed her hand and, as always, it made Destini feel as if everything was going to be all right.

Of course, Dee Dee being Dee Dee, immediately perked up to her usual, jovial self, evidently sensing that she needed to get Destini's mind off her troubles.

"Let's gossip, Destini, shall we?" she suggested, grinning from ear to ear. "Oh, yes, let's gossip. I have some wonderful, juicy gossip that I'm just dying to share with someone."

"Okay," Destini reluctantly agreed, sounding more glum than interested in listening to mindless, meddling rumors. "Lemme hear what you got," she added with a sigh.

"Do you know Noland Newsby, the editor of the Turpricone News? He's tall, has silver hair, kind of patrician looking? He's got those gorgeous baby blues, he's not married, and he has that lady friend, Miss

Traci? You know... she's his partner and she's lived with him for years? Out of wedlock, of course."

"Yes, I know him, or rather, I know of him," Destini said, nodding her head.

"Well, honey, it seems that Mr. Newsby was off on a business trip to just where we came from, New Orleans. Went there by himself about twice a year to some big convention they have for news editors in that town. Anyway, he was staying at a hotel in the French Quarter and Miss Traci decided she'd go down there for a visit and surprise him."

"I think I know where this is going, and it ain't soundin' very good," Destini said, shaking her head, but seeming more interested now.

"No, it's not good, but it's not what you might think, either. In fact, it may just take your breath away, honey."

"Oh, lordie," Destini said, still shaking her head back and forth, as she prepared to hear something truly shocking come out of Dee Dee's mouth.

"Well, Miss Traci went up to the room where he was staying and knocked on the door. No answer," Dee Dee said. "She called his cell phone. Still, no answer. So, she camped out in the lobby, and she waited and she waited, and along about two in the morning, he came strolling in. On his arm was a gorgeous lady, all done up in a purple cocktail dress. She was shapely and beautiful, but upon closer inspection, Miss Traci could see that the lady with Mr. Newsby wasn't a lady at all. It was... wait for it...," she teased her, and then she took a deep breath. "It was a man dressed as a woman."

"Shut up!!" Destini shouted, as her eyes grew wide in utter disbelief. "Oh, my goodness gracious! Just like Carl Alvin used to do when he played Carla Elaine over in Jacksonville!"

"You got it, honey!" Dee Dee shouted. "Needless to say, the Magic City experienced another hurricane that night. In case you were wondering, Miss Traci came home sporting a diamond the size of a hubcap... one that they claim has a dimmer switch on it. It's rumored they will marry sometime this summer."

"Lord have mercy!" Destini said, still a bit flabbergasted, but laughing just the same. "Well, actually, nothing really shocks me anymore, Dee Dee, but that came pretty darn close. Uh-huhh... It sho' did. I'll bet that man is scared to death not to marry her now. She knows too much. She knows *wayyy* too much."

"You got it, cutie-pie," Dee Dee said. "They claim that queen he was with was a famous artist and often impersonated several well-known country and western performers. They also claim there was damn near a killing in the lobby of the hotel that night. It wasn't clear who Miss Traci was going to kill, though; Mr. Newsby or the queen."

Tears were streaming down Destini's face, she was laughing so hard, and so was Dee Dee, but she kept on.

"He swore that he didn't know the queen was a man," Dee Dee said. "Now hold your breath, my darlin' Destini. You'll never guess what her stage name was, so I'll tell ya. It was Beauty Belle! Ha! Can you believe it? Ol' Beauty Belle evidently took exception to Mr. Newsby's denial, since he had been coming to see her… or him… whatever… for the past ten years," Dee Dee added, still laughing.

"Lord Almighty," Destini gasped, still shaking her head. "You just never know, do you? You sho' 'nuff jus' never know."

"No, you never do," Dee Dee said, and then she took a deep breath and cleared her throat. "Okay, I got one more," she added. "One more…"

"I don't know if I can handle another one after that, Miss Dee Dee, but go ahead. I'm listenin'," Destini told her.

"Okay, this next one is about the man who is head of the health department back home," Dee Dee began. "Honey, the reason so much has been, shall we say, put on the back burner is, number one, he really doesn't care much about Campbell County."

"Well, I coulda' tol' you that," Destini interrupted her.

"Just hang on. I'm getting to the good part," Dee Dee said, shushing her with a wave of her hand. "Every time you're around him, he'll let you know in no uncertain terms that he works primarily over in neighboring Alamatta County, and that his primary allegiance is over there. Oh, he makes his little trips back and forth, but like certain religious sects, that shall remain nameless, he always, always travels in pairs. You know... with one of his assistants. I really don't know her name, but everybody calls her Miss Vinceene."

"I do believe I've heard that name bandied about," Destini said.

"Well, Vinceene's arrival for any meeting can always be heard by three distinct things well before you can actually see her," Dee Dee continued. "The clang of her bracelets is one. I swear, the woman wears more bangled bracelets and charms than anyone I've ever known. Number two is the click of her super-high, high heeled shoes banging against the floor. If you watch her, you'll see that she always coyly glances at everyone's feet. If they're the slightest bit wide, she'll get up in their face and swear that her own feet will fit into nothing but a quad A, you know, those super-slim AAAA shoes? Oh, and then she'll let you know that she always has to special-order her shoes."

"Well, la-tee-da to her," Destini said with a sneer. "I dare her to say anything about my big ol' feet."

"I know, right?" Dee Dee agreed, laughing. "It's like, who cares about your darned skinny feet?"

"I sure don't," Destini said.

"Anyway, the third thing is the fog, and I do mean the fog of her perfume," Dee Dee went on. "It smells like ten bushels of gardenias were crushed into a little box all at once and then an added sweetener was thrown in for good measure. Whatever kind of perfume it is, the health department guy, Mr. Derrick Dunceless, seems to love it."

"Oh, my goodness! Is that really his name? Derrick

Dunceless?" Destini asked.

"Well, it's Derrick something," Dee Dee said. "All I know is it sounds like Dunceless, so that's what I'm calling him. Besides, it fits."

"You got that right," Destini agreed.

"I heard when Vinceene talked about moving to another department closer to her home, they had to hospitalize ol' Derrick for nerve troubles. From what I understand, she really knows her job and people say her work is real, even if her boobs are not."

"Ohh, Miss Dee Dee!" Destini gasped.

"Well, it's true," Dee Dee said. "Anyway, the man can't find time to do anything about what's going on with the groundwater in Campbell County, or anything else that has to do with our county because he's too busy running after Miss Skinny Feet."

Destini was laughing at Dee Dee's story, but she was also concerned that no one at the health department seemed to be looking out for the people of Seraph Springs or Campbell County.

"The word on the street is that Derrick's wife... I think her name is Betsy... anyway, I heard she doesn't really care about his little escapades because they supposedly have an open marriage," Dee Dee continued. "She's got some fancy job as financial director for some mental hospital in Fort Allen over near Tallahassee. It's rumored that she's a marathon runner, and has gone through dozens of twenty-something-year-old trainers like a dose of salts through a widow woman, but that's just rumor."

"Gotta love them rumors," Destini interjected.

"The two of them, her and Derrick, have two children; a kind, sweet-looking son, who's in high school, and a daughter, who's kinda like one of those types who love hitting you hard with a dodgeball. Not a pretty girl, at all, bless her heart. She's had her nose done and her little pointed ears clipped, but it hasn't helped. Oh, and she has the most atrocious table manners."

"How do you know that?" Destini asked.

"I witnessed it myself one night at a really nice restaurant in Pittstown," Dee Dee told her. "It was a fundraiser for something over at the university. Honey, I've seen Uncle Hamp's men who worked on log trucks eat with more manners than that girl. By the way, most of those trucker guys, in my book, were gentlemen. I loved them all. Anyway, little Miss Athletic needs a trip to charm school, if you want my opinion. It won't help her looks, but a little polish could do her a world of good. She needs something, that's for sure."

"You ought to be ashamed, Dee Dee," Destini said. "Po lil' girl can't help it if she ain't pretty. Maybe she's really sweet."

"From what I hear, she's about as sweet as a rattlesnake right before it strikes."

"Well, now, that's a different story," Destini said.

"Yep, it was a story, all right," Dee Dee said. "A true one, though."

"Well, girl, you've made me laugh and you got my mind off the bad stuff for a while. For that, I thank you."

"Any time," Dee Dee said, and she reached over to hug her friend.

"I guess we'll be landing before too much longer," Destini said. "I can't wait to get home and see my baby and all the other folks. I love going off to visit, but I'm always glad to get back home."

"We'll have a car waiting for us at the airport to whisk us there, too," Dee Dee said, smiling.

"I guess Miss Sissy still has a lotta pull with the sheriff, huh?"

"Ya think?" Dee Dee rhetorically asked, rolling her eyes. "Well, I'm gonna go freshen my makeup and then rest my eyes for a few minutes before we land."

"Have fun," Destini said. "I'll be sittin' right here waitin' for you."

A short while later, the pilot announced their descent and that they would be landing in about five minutes. When the ladies got off the plane, the first thing Destini spotted was a large banner. On it was written, *Welcome Home, Dee Dee and Destini*, and holding the banner was none other than Nadine, Wanda Faye and Carl Alvin.

"You crazy things!" Dee Dee squealed, as she rushed toward them. "What are y'all doing here?"

After all the hugs and kisses, Nadine replied, "We got a call from the sheriff earlier today. He said he couldn't make it, as he got called away on an emergency. So, Carl Alvin came to the rescue and told us that stretch limo over there could easily hold us all, so we thought, why not? We'll go over and meet you guys and turn it into a little party on the way back home."

"Cool," Dee Dee said.

"We'll catch you up on some news, too," Nadine added.

"Ohh, I am so glad to see you," Destini said to Nadine. "How is my Bunnye? How are all the babies?"

"Honey, they are all just fine," Nadine assured her. "Louie and Dink took them to one of those Christmas movies over in Pittstown, and then they were going out for pizza. They've had a ball while you were gone. When we get back, though, do make a point to comment on how beautiful their Christmas tree is. They've put it up on the side porch of Camp EZ. Whether you think it's pretty or not, just tell them it's gorgeous, okay?"

"Actually, there are two trees," Wanda Faye interjected.

"Two trees?" Destini asked. "Why two? And why so soon? We ain't had Thanksgivin' yet."

"Well, one tree – and believe it or not, it's because of your daughter – is decorated with plastic Easter eggs in honor of her name. All the eggs are either hot pink or purple. No other colors."

"That's my girl," Destini said, smiling wide.

"The other tree, the boys put together," Nadine continued. "It's decorated with camouflage everything! And I mean everything! The lights even look like shotgun shells. It truly is something to behold."

"I'll bet!" Destini said, still smiling, and so happy to hear how well the kids got along while she was away.

"Actually, both trees look really good," Wanda Faye butted in. "Aside from the Easter eggs, Bunnye's tree has all soft pink lights. With the bright green and amber lights on the other tree that the boys did, it doesn't look as bad as it may sound. They kinda go together, if you can believe that."

"Yeah, we had to agree to let them do the two trees to kinda keep 'em off the main tree in the camp," Nadine explained. "You know that tree has to look just perfect with all of Jerri Faye's precious little ornaments and the red velvet bows Mr. Hamp always favored. Quite honestly, it looks just like it did when he was here."

"That's good," Destini said, nodding her head. "That's how it should be. You still ain't told me why y'all are puttin' up Christmas trees so soon."

"Let's just say we needed a distraction and leave it at that, okay?" Nadine explained.

"Gotcha," Destini said. "Now, tell me, how is your mama and how is Essie?"

"Well, Duke called us from the hospital earlier today," Nadine began. "He and Louie went down there, and Brother and Sister Linton were already there with Mama. Me and Wanda Faye didn't go today. We're all kinda taking turns."

"They're both doing better today from what we heard and they might be able to come home in the next couple of days," Wanda Faye said. "They're still having some nausea and there are still a few more tests that have to be run."

"The doctors said they're not sure as to the extent of what's going on, but they should have a better handle on it soon," Nadine said. "When that doctor from up north that Phil Jr. is bringing with him does the tests on the wells, he'll send over the results to the hospital. Then, maybe we'll all know what's causing all this illness."

"I'm so worried about both of them," Destini said, as her eyes welled with tears. "I sure hope they figure this out soon."

"Sooo… what else is going on at home?" Dee Dee asked, as everyone piled into the limo, evidently in an attempt to lighten the mood. "Anything new and interesting?"

"Well, there's some news from down at the health department," Nadine started, as everyone buckled up for the ride home. "Poor, old Miss Jones, who cleans up down there, had to be put in the hospital. Seems her heart ran away from her."

"What you talkin' 'bout, girl?" Destini asked, not knowing whether to laugh or be concerned.

"From what we heard, she went in late Saturday afternoon and was doing her cleaning when she heard a popping sound coming from down the hallway," Nadine explained. "She said she thought something had fallen from one of the shelves or something, but, honey, that wasn't it at all."

"What was it? What was it?" Destini asked, as her

eyes grew wide with anticipation.

"Well, it was Miss Vinceene and she was dressed up like the Lone Ranger, complete with a mask and a cowboy hat, and she was chasing after Mr. Dunceless, who was in a buckskin loin cloth and an Indian head bonnet."

"Ohhh! Lord have mercy!" Destini gasped, as she doubled over in laughter.

"He was painted all over in war paint, and she was shootin' those guns and popping that cap pistol," Nadine continued. "Miss Jones said what she saw through the opened door of one of the exam rooms, though, was… well, it made the poor thing faint! Let's just say the cowboy had conquered the Indian!" Nadine ended, laughing as hard as Destini and everyone else now.

Once everybody calmed down, Wanda Faye shouted, "Okay, let's have a drink! Charge us up, Carl Alvin! Our girls are home!"

"You betcha!" Carl Alvin replied, and then he popped open a bottle of champagne.

All the way back to Seraph Springs, the entire group had one laughing spell after the next, as they caught up on all the latest gossip and went through three bottles of champagne. In the back of Destini's mind, though, were thoughts and worries about Miss Jewell and Essie. The expressions in the eyes of Nadine and Wanda Faye didn't fool her. She could tell they were as worried as she was, even though they were putting on a good front.

There was one thing Destini knew for certain. She meant to get to the bottom of what was causing folks in Campbell County to get sick, and she was going to walk the effort each step of the way if she had to.

She started humming to herself, and then she told the girls that since she was home again, she felt like singing.

"Well, sing it, girl!" Nadine prodded her, and so she did.

"Mary, don't you weep,
Martha, don't you moan no more,
I said, Miss Mary… don't you weep,
Tell Martha not to moan no more.

Pharaoh's army,
Got drowned in the sea one day.
Mary, Mary, don't you weep,
Tell Martha not to moan.
Now if I could, I surely would,
Stand on the rock where Moses stood.

Pharaoh's army,
Got drowned in the sea one day.
Mary, don't you weep,
Tell Martha not to moan."

෪෪෪෪෪෪෪෪෪෪

IT WAS FAIRLY late, and well after sundown by the

time the group arrived at Camp EZ, but on the surface one might think it was the middle of the day as bright as it was. Every light in the place was burning. When the limousine pulled up to the entrance, the children ran outside to greet them, as if they had been standing watch at the window. Bunnye, of course, was leading the crowd.

After all the hugs and kisses, and some catching up, it was time for everyone to think about getting some shuteye. Wanda Faye and Nadine gathered up all their kids and headed home and the limousine took Carl Alvin and Dee Dee, to their respective homes.

Destini and Bunnye headed upstairs. Once Bunnye brushed her teeth, Destini came in and tucked her in, before retreating to her own bedroom.

She prayed long and hard for Essie and Miss Jewell before going to sleep that night. She asked the Lord if it was his will to heal them, and to give her the wisdom and knowledge to find out what was making her friends and relatives so ill. After her prayers, she recalled the dream she had in New Orleans and she knew she needed to talk to Mama Tee as soon as possible.

As she lay there in bed, an odd sense of comfort swept over her and she smiled, just knowing she was safe at home with her beautiful daughter soundly sleeping down the hallway. After all, home is where she felt most comfortable and Camp EZ was definitely home, sweet home to her in so many ways.

"I can face anything here," she thought, smiling, as she drifted off to sleep.

Chapter 18

Destini was up bright and early the next morning, thanks to the two old bantam roosters inside the barn that were crowing their hearts out at the break of day. Since she couldn't go back to sleep, she figured she may as well go downstairs and put some coffee on.

"Dang, this tummy of mine is givin' me a fit," she said, as she descended the stairs. "I sure hope I ain't comin' down with this sickness."

While the coffee was brewing, she threw a few slabs of bacon into a frying pan and mixed up a batch of biscuits. She was on her second cup of the savory black medicine, watching the biscuits turn a light brown color inside the oven, when Bunnye came bounding down the stairs.

"Well, good mornin', sweetie. You look cheerful today," Destini said.

Bunnye was already dressed for school, which, quite frankly, shocked Destini, as it was completely out of the norm.

"Mornin', Mama," Bunnye said, and then she planted a kiss on her mother's cheek. "Ooh! I'll make the eggs!" she offered. "I love to make eggs!"

"I know you do, my little cherub," Destini said, returning her kiss, and then nearly breaking down into tears, as she realized her little girl was growing up. "Don't forget, I like mine a little runny, okay?" she added.

"Okay, Mama," Bunnye said. "I'll make 'em good. Don't you worry."

Destini went over to the counter to pour herself another cup of coffee, hoping it would calm her stomach. She happened to glance out the window and saw plumes of dust being kicked up along the roadway, as several cars pulled up to the entrance of the camp.

"Well, shut my mouth," she mumbled, shaking her head when she recognized who it was. "Bunnye, it looks like we got some company. You'd better get some more eggs out, honey. Oh, and throw some more bacon in that skillet, too. A lot more. I forgot everyone was coming over here this morning," she added, still shaking her head and chastising herself for not remembering.

Moments later, Nadine and Wanda Faye walked into the lodge carrying grocery bags full of food. Behind them were all their kids; Little Chet, Victor Newman, John Lewis, Jewell Lee, Little Hamp, Charlene, Darlene, and Dale Earnhardt.

"I'll do the grits," Wanda Faye offered, without even saying hello first.

"I'll help Bunnye with the eggs," Nadine said. "You kids go watch some TV until breakfast is ready. You can go too, Bunnye. I can take care of this."

"That's okay, Miss Nadine. I like cooking eggs. Right, Mama?" Bunnye asked.

"That's right, my sweet baby," Destini said, and then she tried to grab some plates from the cupboard, but she was shooed away by Wanda Faye.

"There's too many cooks in this kitchen, Destini. Why don't you go out to my car and bring in those jars of mayhaw jelly and fig preserves?" Wanda Faye practically ordered her. "Bring that newspaper in, too. You might want to read it."

"Yes, ma'am," Destini said, saluting her, as if she was her commanding officer.

A few minutes later, when she returned to the kitchen and looked at the front page of the *Turpricone News,* her eyes widened. She immediately sat down at the kitchen table to read. The headline stated:

Federal agency probes possible groundwater contamination around Seraph Springs and throughout Campbell County.

The article went on at length about the numbers of tainted wells that had been discovered in the county, and the further discovery of something amiss in the groundwater. *Feed the World Organics,* the fairly new farming enterprise on the outskirts of Seraph Springs, was at the center of the investigation, from what Destini could gather.

"There's that name again, Dimitri Smith," she thought, as she read.

According to the article, Dimitri Smith wasn't real happy at the moment. It seemed *Feed the World Organics* had filed numerous complaints over the last several months about the water that was being pumped through their irrigation systems, and how some of their produce had failed inspection because of high levels of toxicity.

"Wow," was all Destini could manage to say at the moment.

"Check out page three under letters to the editor," Wanda Faye told her. "He's still goin' at it."

"Who?" Destini asked.

"You'll see," Wanda Faye said, grinning.

There had been numerous letters to the editor on the tainted groundwater subject recently, mostly from Seraph Springs' own resident malcontent, Josiah E. Emoryceil, whose ignorance threatened to downplay the seriousness of the situation.

Over the past few decades, Josiah had solicited more public records requests to the local government than any human, alive or dead. That was his trademark and the entire county tried their best to avoid contact with him, lest they become his next target.

It didn't matter who was holding office in either the county or the city government because ol' Josiah could dream up slanderous diatribes against any of them. He seemed to feel no shame in publicly embarrassing anyone, no matter who they were. He would constantly verbalize his vile thoughts to anyone who would dare to listen. He also changed his allegiances more than the weather changed in north Florida, so most folks didn't pay him too much mind. All his little placards, his notes, and his slights against people were laughable at times, but in the end he was just a nuisance, plain and simple.

Josiah even published his own little newspaper, not that he had that many loyal readers. Most folks just read it to get their day's worth of entertainment, as he falsely professed to be such a wise and educated man. If one dared to ask him if he had a theology or psychology degree, or if he had really been a minister at some point in his life, which he claimed he was, well... it all depended on the day you asked him as to what answer you'd get. Oftentimes, you could find him standing on the corners in downtown Seraph Springs screaming about hellfire and damnation, while denouncing the sins of others, and all the while claiming he was the blessed messiah.

Sometimes he rode around on his little motorized scooter and sometimes he walked or even skipped. It all depended on whether or not he wanted folks to believe he was truly terribly physically disabled. It was the general consensus of most of Campbell County's residents that he was a weirdo in the first degree. One day, he had screamed at Carl Alvin and told him he was one of the most gender-confused people in the world.

Carl Alvin had retorted with, "You bet your bippy, sweetcakes, but you are just plain crazy! Every village has an idiot, and you are ours!"

Even now, as Destini read another of his idiotic, senseless letters to the editor, she couldn't help but laugh to herself.

"Well, good morning, ladies," Dee Dee cheerfully

chirped, as she joined the group in the kitchen. "How's everybody doing this morning?"

"What are you so happy about?" Nadine asked her. "Here… have some coffee," she added, and she handed her a mug of Destini's special brew. "We're all still trying to wake up."

"Well, I am wide awake," Dee Dee proudly said, and she snatched the newspaper from Destini's hands.

"Hey! I was reading that!" Destini yelled.

"And now I'm reading it," Dee Dee said, smiling as she quickly rifled through the pages, and acting just like the queen bee that Mama Tee had described yesterday.

"Whatever," Destini said, with a heavy sigh.

"By the way, Carl Alvin should be here any minute. I just talked to him on his cell phone," Dee Dee said. "Oh! Look here, girls!" she shouted. "On page eight it says Doughnut Dawson is gonna cook Christmas dinner for the governor."

Destini rolled her eyes. "Ol' Doughnut? Now, Dee Dee, you know his name is Cyril Darrow Dawson."

"Yes, I know, silly," Dee Dee said, rolling her eyes back at Destini. "I know all about his nationally renowned cookbooks and that he's known as Chef Cyril. What's that show he does? Cooking with Chef Cyril?" she asked, scrunching up her face.

"That would be correct," Destini said.

"Well, all I remember is us chasing the poor thing when we were kids and watching as his boobs bounced around from all the fat he carried around with him," Dee Dee said, laughing.

"Yeah, and we'd squeeze those big boobs, and then suck in our breath and yell, "Titty twister!", and he'd get all freaked out and scream like a little baby," Nadine interjected.

Now everyone in the kitchen was doubled over in laughter.

"Look at him now, though," Destini said, once everyone calmed down. "He's cooking for rock stars and celebrities."

"He's still the same old Doughnut," Dee Dee piped up. "Wantin' the world to think he's somebody special. Gosh, his photos are everywhere and he's on all those cooking shows. The one thing I remember that still cracks me up is when Carl Alvin gave that fool homemade fudge one year for his birthday. It was all done up in that beautifully wrapped box, too."

"Ohh, I remember that, too," Nadine said. "He put a laxative in the fudge. A lot of it!"

"Yep, poor Doughnut," Dee Dee said. "I think it was one of the few times he actually lost some weight."

"I think you're right," Nadine agreed.

"Remember that hateful Celesta Wesson?" Dee Dee asked the girls. "You know… Judge Wesson's niece, who used to come here and visit from Savannah? Well, she was at the grocery store last year when Doughnut came in with his entourage that included his trainer, who had more caps on his teeth than any toothpaste ad I ever saw. Doughnut was wearing one of them topnotch hairpieces, 'cause you know he's going bald, right? Oh, and Celeste had on dark sunglasses because she was probably hung over," she added, seemingly wound up like a chatterbox this morning for some reason. "Anyway, it was about two in the afternoon, so she probably hadn't been up long at all, and she was thumbing through a magazine she grabbed off the rack. You could tell that Doughnut didn't want her to recognize him 'cause he was kinda sneakin' around the aisles. She saw him, though, and when she did, she didn't speak. She screamed at him!"

"What did she say?" Destini asked.

"She didn't say, she yelled, "Doughnut! Well, I'll be damned! You have fallen off, really lost some weight, sweetie! Your face is still long as a billy goat, but gosh, Doughnut, you're lookin' better!" Then she lowered her voice a bit, said it was good to see him, and she wished him a merry Christmas."

"Oh, my word," Destini said. "What did he do?"

"He rolled his eyes, and said, "The name is Cyril, honey." To which she replied, "The name is Doughnut, Doughnut, and unless you want me to tell these people how you left a trail of doo-doo at our fifth grade Christmas party after you ate that laxative-laced chocolate fudge, we'd better leave the pretensions for the cooking channels, sweetness."

Destini's jaw dropped, but she laughed, as she tried to picture it all happening.

"She wasn't done yet, though," Dee Dee went on. "She told him, "You know, Doughnut, you've done well for yourself, you have. For someone who couldn't spell the word sugar or cup or butter... I'll be damned if you haven't done well. Congratulations. My best to your mama, too. One of the sweetest folks alive." Can y'all believe that woman?!" Dee Dee asked.

Again, the whole group laughed until they cried.

Just then, Mama Tee and Sister Violet walked into the kitchen. It was about two minutes before seven now and they were right on time, just as they said they would be.

"What's all the commotion about?" Sister Violet asked.

"Oh, nothin', sweetie," Destini told her. "Just havin' a few laughs this mornin'. Bunnye, you got Mama Tee's plate ready?"

"Yes, Mama," Bunnye replied, and she carefully placed a plate of eggs, bacon, grits and a buttered biscuit down on the table in front of Mama Tee.

"Here's you some coffee," Nadine said, and she handed Mama Tee a mug of the steaming brew.

"You got Violet her plate?" Mama Tee asked.

"Now, Mama Tee, you know we done took care of Sister Violet. She's fine," Nadine assured her, as she placed Violet's plate on the table.

"Jus' checking," the old woman said. "How about my baby, Phil? Is he here yet?"

"Not yet, Mama Tee," Destini said.

At that precise moment, there was a knocking on the back door and, lo and behold, it was Phil. He went first over to Mama Tee and kissed her on the forehead. Then he walked over to Destini, who rolled her eyes at him.

"I know you better be givin' me some of that sugar, as many times as I kept you," Destini teased him, and he laughed.

"You know wherever the two of you are is home for me," he said. "It's so good to see you, Destini."

"Well, you have a seat," Destini told him. "Bunnye, would you make a plate for Phil, please?"

"Already done, Mama," Bunnye proudly said, and she handed him his plate. "Would you like some coffee?" she asked him.

"Yes, I would," he said. "Thank you, Bunnye." He turned to Destini and whispered, "You've done a good job with that little girl. You should be proud."

"I am proud," Destini assured him. "I'm very proud of my baby girl."

"Well, look what the cat drug in," Dee Dee announced, when Carl Alvin entered the room. "What took you so long?"

"Don't ask," he mumbled, as he tugged on the collar of his shirt, which seemed to have a mind of its own this morning, as it just wouldn't lay flat.

"We'll be ready in just a little while, Phil," Wanda Faye said, as she took her dirty dishes over to the sink. "We need to get these children off to school first and then we'll head down to the hospital as soon as we get back."

"That's fine," he said. "It will give Carl Alvin and me some time to eat."

"Well, at least someone is looking out for me," Carl Alvin snorted to Dee Dee. "Nadine, I'll take mine over easy, please."

"Comin' right up," Nadine said.

"I want to thank you again for driving us, Phil," Destini said. "It means a lot... to all of us."

"It is my pleasure," Phil said, and he reached over to squeeze Destini's hand. "There's plenty of room in my van for all eight of us to sit comfortably. Plus, it will give us more time to catch up on things by riding down there together. By the way, these eggs are absolutely delicious," he added, and he shot Bunnye a huge smile.

Bunnye smiled back at him and mouthed a thank you, as Destini looked on, thinking again how grown up her little girl was.

Chapter 19

On the way to the hospital in Gainesville, the entire group chit-chatted about the article in the paper referencing the federal probe into claims of groundwater contamination in Campbell County. Phil advised everyone that his friend, Dr. David Hoffman, had been given permission by Essie and Miss Jewell to analyze their test results that had been collected over the past several days while they'd been hospitalized.

"David studied medicine at Cornell University School of Medicine, as well as Johns Hopkins," Phil explained. "I have a feeling the test results will be quite informative."

Upon arrival at the hospital about an hour later, and without warning of any kind, Dee Dee and Carl Alvin suddenly grabbed onto each other and both of them started crying like babies. In fact, Carl Alvin was almost inconsolable.

Destini knew what was going on in their heads, even if the others didn't. It had been some time since Mr. Hamp's death, but the last time Dee Dee and Carl Alvin had been to the Gainesville hospital was the day their beloved uncle died. It took a few minutes, but they finally calmed down, thanks to Mama Tee's suggestion they all form a circle, hold hands and say a few words of prayer.

"Mama Tee always knows what to do," Destini thought, as everyone made their way up to the entrance of the hospital.

Once the group made it inside and loaded into one of the lobby elevators, Phil pushed the button for the third floor. By unanimous consent, Nadine, Wanda Faye, Dee Dee and Carl Alvin were going to visit Miss Jewell first, while Phil, Destini, Mama Tee and Sister Violet would go to Essie's room at the other end of the corridor.

ॐॐॐॐॐॐॐॐॐॐ

AS WANDA FAYE, Nadine, Dee Dee and Carl Alvin were approaching Miss Jewell's room, Brother and Sister Linton's voices could be heard out in the hallway. They were praying quite loudly, and as the group entered the room, Sister Linton ended the prayer by saying, "Amen and amen."

When Miss Jewell spotted her two daughters standing in the doorway, she immediately broke down into tears, and then reached out to embrace them both. Then, it was Dee Dee's turn and then Carl Alvin's.

"Mama, how are you feeling today?" Nadine asked. "Your color looks a lot better."

"Yes, you're looking good and rested, Miss Jewell," Dee Dee added.

"Bless your hearts, my little angels," Miss Jewell told them. "I know I must look like death warmed over, though."

"You look beautiful," Carl Alvin told her, which made her smile.

"Anyway, Dee Dee, are you getting things ready for your wedding?" Miss Jewell asked. "It seems like a long ways away, but it'll be here before you know it. Now, you do know I'm going to be making your cake, don't you?"

"Absolutely, I know it!" Dee Dee exclaimed, all smiles. "I wouldn't dream of having anyone else make my wedding cake, Miss Jewell, and the groom's cake, too, for that matter. I want plenty of those delicious cakes you make for the rehearsal dinner, as well. That means you need to get better real quick, ya hear? We need you there to make all the cakes."

"Unless I fall over and die between now and then, I'll be at your wedding, honey, with however many cakes your little heart desires. You can count on it," Miss Jewell assured her.

❧ ❧ ❧ ❧ ❧ ❧ ❧ ❧ ❧ ❧

ABOUT FIFTEEN MINUTES later, Phil came down to Miss Jewell's room and motioned for Dee Dee to come out into the corridor.

"What's up?" she asked.

"Would you grab the others and join the rest of us in the conference room?" he asked her. "It's just down the hall on the right."

"Sure," she said. "Is everything okay?"

"Just bring everyone into the conference room as soon as you can," he told her, and he turned and started back down the corridor.

"We'll be right there!" she called after him, and she went back inside Miss Jewell's room.

In the conference room minutes later, Phil directed everyone to take a seat around a huge, carved oak, oval desk in the middle of the spacious room. A few moments later, Dr. Hoffman arrived. The man was well over six feet tall in stature and extremely handsome, Destini thought, even though he was obviously going bald with only a few curly tendrils left near his temples.

Destini watched Dee Dee out of the corner of her eye and noticed she gave the doctor her gaga-eyed stamp of approval. Wanda Faye and Nadine, who were sitting beside her, followed suit.

"Dang crazy women," Destini thought, as she quietly chuckled to herself. "I swear, I ain't never seen such a bunch of grown women actin' like teenagers, drooling over a man like that."

Meanwhile, Phil, who was sitting next to Destini, was blushing as red as a beet.

"Gee, can you tell they're southern girls?" he whispered to Destini.

"Ahem," Destini grunted, and then she kicked Dee Dee in the shins underneath the table.

"What?" Dee Dee mouthed, looking across the table at Destini with her eyes crossed and a big grin on her face.

That's when Destini reached over and grabbed

Phil's left hand. She pointed to his ring, and then pointed over at Dr. Hoffman, but all Dee Dee did was shrug her shoulders and grin even wider.

Dr. Hoffman seemed to have picked up on something because he asked Dee Dee, "Is there anything I can help you with?"

"Oh, my," Dee Dee began, pretending she was embarrassed all of a sudden. "I think I'm beginning to feel the vapors coming on," she said, batting her eyes at him. "If I faint, Dr. Hoffman, will you catch me?" she added with a huge smile.

Everyone laughed, including Dr. Hoffman, who was now blushing as much as Phil.

"Thank you for that, Mrs....?" Dr. Hoffman trailed off.

"It's Miss... Miss Dee Dee Wilson," she said, still trying to flirt with him.

"Soon to be Mrs. Ricardo Fernandez," Destini piped up. "She's just a born flirt, Dr. Hoffman. Don't pay her no mind. We do appreciate you takin' time to talk with us today," she added, and then Dee Dee shot her a hateful glance.

"You're quite welcome," Dr. Hoffman said. "Now, moving right along... I realize that agriculture and the farming industry have been a huge presence in Campbell County for quite some time. Probably more now than ever, since *Feed the World Organics* arrived on the scene. However, do any of you recall anything else ever being on any portion of that property where those new farms are located, other than just the old farms that used to be there? The reason I ask is because of what I have discovered in the biopsies taken from Miss Jewell and Miss Essie. By the way, Miss Jewell has shown me her cross from the Holy Land and also had your pastor lay hands on me, so I am good to go," he added with a smile, which gave everyone a good laugh.

"That's our mama," Nadine said, smiling, as she took hold of Wanda Faye's hand.

"On a more serious note, and back to my question, do any of you know if there was ever any large dry cleaning establishment anywhere close to those new farms at any time in the past?" the doctor asked.

"Not that I'm aware of," Dee Dee said, and then everyone else in the room shook their heads in agreement, except two people.

"I know of one person who could probably answer your question," Phil said, and he looked over at Mama Tee, who was sitting to his left.

"Mama Tee, do you remember anything about a dry cleaning operation near where those new farms are?" he asked her, speaking loud and clear, so that she would understand the question.

"Oh, yes, honey," she said. "And you don't have to yell. I can hear you jus' fine."

"I'm sorry, Mama Tee," he said. "Please go on."

"Well, it was on the old Jarrellson Plantation," she began. "Lots of us worked there durin' the Second World War. It was a huge place there that made military uniforms. They also dry cleaned the uniforms for lots o' folks who wasn't far from us at Camp

Salisbury. Yeah, it was a big money thing the Jarrellsons arranged through their Congressman at that time," she went on. "Lawd, that place operated twelve, fourteen hours a day! And smell? My goodness! That dry cleanin' stuff they used would just about knock you out. I used to work in the room where the buttons and thangs was sewed on."

"Mrs. Wilson…" Dr. Hoffman started, but Mama Tee interrupted him.

"You listen here, now," she scolded him. "Is you a friend of my baby, Phil?" she asked.

Dr. Hoffman laughed and said, "Yes, I am."

"Then you call me Mama Tee. That's what everyone calls me, as long as they be my friend."

"All right, then, Mama Tee," he said. "Can you tell me what they did with the fluid they used to clean the uniforms after they were done with it?"

"Oh, yes, honey," she said. "They ran most of it through a pipe that went right into that little creek on the Jarrellson place. Lots of it ran into the Suwannee River, and lots of it, well, they just had mens who poured it on the ground. Didn't matter where. They jus' poured it."

"Really? Approximately where was all this going on?" he asked.

"It was on some property down the road a piece between where Miss Jewell lives and my place," Mama Tee said. "You know… where them new farms is. For years in that creek you couldn't catch a fish or even see a little minnow. Folks fish there today, but I never have. No sir-ree. I know what went into that creek."

"Have you been down to that creek lately?" Phil asked her.

"Last time was prob'ly about a month ago when Duke and Essie took me by there," Mama Tee said. "That ol' Wilson Creek where it run in da river? Well, I felt as if I was smellin' that same ol' dry cleanin' plant all over again. It was almost da same smell, but it was fresh this time, like it just been poured in da river, you know?"

"I understand," Dr. Hoffman said.

"Long time after they closed up shop, I started fishing there again ever' once in a while, till not too long ago when Duke saw dem dead soft shelled cooters on the bank of da creek. Then, them gators what was eatin' dem cooters died, and some of dem buzzards that ate 'em died, too. Duke say, "Mama Tee, I think we better stick to da lakes on Mr. Hamp's place or the little pond on da farm." I believes Duke be right. Somethin' goin' on in dat water again. They thought I was crazy when I told 'em 'bout da smell, but I ain't crazy."

"No, you're not," Dr. Hoffman said. "Thank you so much, Mrs.…. I mean, Mama Tee. I certainly hope Phil will bring me by your place one day soon," Dr. Hoffman said.

"Yer welcome," she said, and then she turned to Phil. "Baby, bring this nice man by my house for a visit. He seem like a nice man. Talk kinda like Mr. Stanley Williams. He from up nawth?"

"Yes, ma'am, he's from up north," Phil said, with a chuckle.

"Well, I ain't got one thing against the nawth," Mama Tee went on. "Don't wanna live there, but when I could see, honey, I went up to Harlem one time in the late thirties wid my cousins. Ohh, we had us a time up there. Good music. Lots o' big buildings. Yes, indeed. You realize them nawthern folks freed us, don't you? Say what you want, but they's a lot to be said for that."

"One last question, Mama Tee, if I may," Dr. Hoffman interrupted. "May I ask how old you are?"

"Ohh, lawdy!" she exclaimed, and then she started laughing. "Don't you know you never s'pose to ask a woman her age?"

"She'll be one-hundred-and-two years of age, if she makes it to April first," Destini butted in. "She said she was born on April Fool's Day, and that's why she always enjoys laughter. She gots a good mem'ry, too."

"That, she does," the doctor said. "Now… back to business. The biopsies taken from Miss Jewell and Essie are from small tumors on their livers."

There was a collective gasp from most everyone in the room at that revelation. Nadine and Wanda Faye grasped onto each other's hands again and soon everyone around the table was holding onto each other.

"Now, don't be alarmed," Dr. Hoffman said. "The news I have for you is good news, actually, but I do have some concerns. The good news is that neither Mrs. Wilson nor Mrs. Lee… sorry, I mean Essie and Miss Jewell… are in a life threatening situation. The tumors have been removed, and when tested, no malignancies were found."

"Oh, thank God," Destini said.

"However, this is what we did find," Dr. Hoffman went on. "There were high levels of toxins in the initial biopsies we took, and we know that these toxic chemicals are used primarily in agricultural insecticides and pesticides, which is why I'm asking so many questions. There were also trace amounts of other toxins, which is why I asked about the dry cleaning plant. The thing that bothers me is this. I know *Feed the World Organics* had to have done some testing near the site where the major farming is taking place. I mean, that's just standard operating procedure. I also know now that those two fields in the back are where the old dry cleaning plant used to be."

"Yep, that sounds about right," Mama Tee said.

"I simply don't understand why in the world, at some point in time, no one bothered to clean up the site or at least have the state or federal government get involved in the cleanup," Dr. Hoffman continued. "Even though Miss Jewell and Essie are in no imminent danger at the moment, I would suggest that their wells… or even if someone has a well within ten miles of those two back fields… well, if it was me, I would have the water tested."

The room was silent all of a sudden. Destini swore she could hear everyone's brains churning around in their skulls, including in her own head.

"That is probably the reason those foreign

investors who bought all that property for farming are experiencing some crop failures," Dr. Hoffman continued. "Those deep center pivot irrigation systems have evidently struck on a stream of water that is still highly contaminated. That is my guess, anyway."

There was still complete silence in the room, as everyone tried to digest what the doctor was suggesting.

"Your loved ones are very fortunate," he went on. "Many times, exposure to these chemicals over long periods of time can cause major health problems; sometimes liver cancer, as well as other cancers, and oftentimes a host of other medical problems. I would say all of us here have something for which to be thankful, although, there may be others who aren't so thankful. At any rate, I think Phil and his group from up in Washington have their work cut out for them, and it may be difficult work. I doubt they'll get much cooperation from the farming company, and they probably won't get a lot of cooperation from the local county government, either."

With that, Phil stood up and thanked the doctor for his presentation. Carl Alvin was the first to shake the doctor's hand, followed by everyone else in the room, except Dee Dee, that is.

Ever the zany and ultimate extrovert, she said to him, "Oh, Doctor Feelgood, Doctor Lookgood from up in Yankee-land, I simply must have a hug. And don't worry, we won't tell your wife."

Both Dr. Hoffman and Phil flushed more than just

a little, which made it even funnier to those who were looking on.

Dee Dee hugged the good doctor and said, "My word, if I weren't an engaged woman and you weren't married, honey, I would most assuredly be after you."

"Dee Dee, for gosh sakes, behave yourself, you brazen thing," Destini chastised her, and then she took hold of Dr. Hoffman's hands. "From my heart, I thank you. I do. I do thank you." Then, she turned to Phil. "Little Phil, baby, let me hold you and kiss you. I do want to do that. If it weren't for you, we wouldn't be any closer to knowing what was wrong with our loved ones."

She held out her arms and Phil, the educated, refined, well-traveled young man, fell into the same arms where he had felt such abundant love as a child. As she cradled him and the tears ran down her cheeks, she said, "Thank you, Jesus. Thank you, Lord."

She couldn't see it, but tears were streaming down Phil's face, too, as she held him. Moments later, she addressed the doctor again.

"I guess we'll go back and visit with Essie and Miss Jewell now," Destini said. "I want you to come and have dinner with us, Dr. Hoffman, when it's convenient for you, that is."

"You tell me when it's convenient," he said, smiling. "I've heard all about how well you ladies cook from Phil, but I think he must have been overestimating just a little," he jokingly added.

"You think so?" Destini asked, feigning

belligerence. "Well, you come out to Camp EZ day after tomorrow about five in the afternoon, and we'll just see if you still think Phil is overestimating after you eat some of our cookin'."

"I'd be delighted," he said. "By the way, I understand, Ms. Wilson..."

"It's Destini, honey," she interrupted him. "Just Destini. My baby over there, little Phil, has always called me Destini, and you can, too."

"Okay, Destini. I understand you knew Dr. Watson Williams."

"Knew him? Honey, like Phil here, little Watson was mine for a number of years. I helped raise that young man."

"I knew Watson when I did some work in China," Dr. Hoffman said. "He was working there, too, and I remember hearing he was so in love with a Chinese girl who later died unexpectedly. She was beautiful, I was told. He loved China, and I think he would have stayed there forever had it not been for the new hospital administrator who came in. It seemed Watson lost his way after that and just wandered for a long time. I heard he drank quite heavily for a while, but later got better, married, and had a little girl. I was so sorry to hear of his death. I had dinner with him and his wife once in London. One of the most beautiful ladies I have ever seen."

"Ahem..." Dee Dee mumbled, while clearing her throat at the same time.

"Present company excluded, of course," the doctor

said, blushing a bit as he smiled at Dee Dee.

"I'm glad you got to meet Watson," Destini said. "He was the first baby I ever kept," she added, trying to interrupt the flirting that was going on between Dee Dee and the good doctor. "I still miss him to this day. He had such a kind heart," she went on.

"You know..." Carl Alvin butted in. "I met a young man in New Orleans about three years ago and his name was... hmmm, let me see... Oh! Now I remember! It was Monty Wu. He was working as a bartender at one of the nicer hotels in the French Quarter... Amerasian something or other. Anyway, he and I started talking and the town of Seraph Springs came up. He asked if I had ever known Watson Williams."

"Wow, small world, huh?" the doctor interjected.

"Yeah," Carl Alvin said. "Anyway, he told me he worked at the rehab facility where Watson was a patient after he came back from China. Then he told me all about his unfortunate bout with pills and alcohol."

"Oh, that's right," Destini said. "I remember hearing about that guy. He and Watson became closer than they should have at a time when Watson was so vulnerable. That's when he tried to extort money from my dear, sweet boy. I heard that Monty guy was more or less paid off, and then he left the rehab center in a big ol' hurry."

"Really?" Carl Alvin asked, with a raise of the eyebrows. "I simply recall that he was a handsome young man, but then, the next time I went into that hotel bar, I heard that Monty, too, had become addicted to prescription medications. According to the rumor mill, he was really strung out for a while on cocaine and crystal meth. According to the concierge, who's been working at the hotel for years, Monty overdosed one day and had to be life-flighted out to a trauma center."

"Well, then," Destini smugly said. "Maybe there is some justice in the world, after all. Will y'all excuse me for just a minute?" she asked, as her face turned an awful shade of green.

She hurried as fast as she could to the ladies room across the hall, afraid she wasn't going to make it in time. As she stood inside one of the stalls, all she could think was that she had never felt as sick to her stomach as she did right now, other than the time she was pregnant with Bunnye.

Following close behind her into the restroom were Nadine and Wanda Faye. They made it inside just in time to hear Destini puke up her guts in a violent fashion. Then, Dee Dee pushed through the doorway moments later.

"What is wrong with you, honey?" Wanda Faye asked when Destini emerged from the stall. "My goodness, you look terrible."

"I don't know," Destini said, as she wiped her mouth with a wad of toilet paper. "I'm just not feeling good at all. Actually, I haven't really felt like myself since I got back from New Orleans. At first, I thought it might be all that rich food I ate, but now, I'm not so sure. Last night I got the cold sweats and then I ran a temperature. I can't seem to hold a lot down in my stomach, either."

"Do you think you might be pregnant?" Nadine asked.

Destini laughed so hard that she almost fell over.

"Honey chil', if I be pregnant, then it most assuredly be divine intervention, as I ain't been with no man since... well, since I had Bunnye."

"Destini, honey, I know a really good internist in Jacksonville," Dee Dee interrupted. "His wife and I are great friends. I'm going to make an appointment for you to see him. You need to see someone, sweetheart."

"Uhhh... excuse me, but have you forgotten where we are right now?" Wanda Faye asked Dee Dee. "This is a hospital, you know."

"I know, but I really like this doctor over in Jacksonville. He's one of the best," Dee Dee explained.

"Y'all are makin' a big fuss over nothin'," Destini said. "I'm feelin' better already. Let's just get on home."

"We can do that," Dee Dee said. "I'm still calling the doctor, though, to make you an appointment."

"Whatever, girl," Destini said, shaking her head. "Come on, let's get outta here. I had me about enough hospitals for one day."

After the gang said their goodbyes to Miss Jewell and Essie, they all piled into the elevator again to head down to the lobby. Once outside, Dee Dee pulled out her cell phone and dialed the doctor's number.

After she spoke to him and hung up, she turned to Destini and said, "He will see you the day after tomorrow."

"Wow, that soon?" Destini asked.

"No time like the present, honey," Dee Dee told her, and she put her arm around her shoulder, as they walked to the van.

Out of the corner of her eye, Destini could see Nadine and Wanda Faye looking at each other, as if they were thinking the worst. Now, even she was beginning to think something was terribly wrong with her.

Chapter 20

Destini was sitting in the waiting room of the medical office of Dr. Austin Tucker over in Jacksonville. Dr. Tucker had examined her a week ago and ordered a battery of tests. She was back now to get the results. In the waiting room with her was Dee Dee.

Just last night, Destini had talked to Mama Tee about her dream and the old woman's words hung over her like a thick fog now. Mama Tee had closed her eyes and gone into a trance, it seemed. Then, she told her exactly what the dream meant, and Destini trusted her words, as if they were scripture.

"Honey, the part about them deer comin' to the water to drink, and then fallin' over... well, I ain't real sure on that one, but I believe all it means is they's folks in your life who care about you. Now, the part about the ducks... two of 'em jus' disappearin' like that? Honey, I'm afraid it's about some people close to you who's gonna die soon."

"Really, Mama Tee?" Destini asked, suddenly wishing she hadn't even brought up the dream.

"Yes, chil'," the old woman said. "One of 'em is gonna leave this earth with a lil' bit 'o warnin', but the other one will be leavin' suddenly... very suddenly, and it will be a shock to everyone."

Then, Mama Tee did something she seldom ever did. She dropped her chin to her chest and she cried. Then, she held her chest, and said, "My heart feels so heavy. I feel so tired."

Mama Tee had never complained about her health before and it made Destini wonder if she was talking about herself when she was explaining the dream. For several minutes, she watched as tears ran down her grandmother's wrinkled face and it made her sad... very, very sad.

"Ms. Wilson, the doctor will see you now," the receptionist called out across the waiting room.

Dr. Tucker appeared in the doorway leading to the exam rooms and he was holding someone's chart in his hands. He nodded to Destini as she got closer and the expression on his face was completely unreadable, she thought.

She asked if Dee Dee could come into the exam room with her while he shared the results of her tests.

"Of course, if you wish," he said, and still, his facial expression never changed. "Follow me," he added, and he turned and started walking down the long corridor to his office.

"Ms. Wilson, the news I have for you today is not good," he began, as soon as he sat down behind his desk. "I wish it could be better, but it's not good. You have cancer. It is stage four. It is in the liver and the pancreas," he said, showing no emotion as he spoke.

"What did you say?" Destini asked, clearly dumbfounded, as her eyes widened in disbelief.

Dee Dee, who could normally handle stressful situations like this with ease, reached for Destini's hand and squeezed it tight.

"Once again, you have cancer," Dr. Tucker repeated. "It is stage four. It is in the liver and the pancreas... and it is widespread," he added. "I have a colleague in this office who is an oncologist, Dr. Abraham Wettstein, who will come in and talk with you in a few moments about treatment possibilities."

"How much time?" Destini wanted to know.

"None of us can know that for sure, Ms. Wilson, but I will let Dr. Wettstein talk to you more about that."

"Well, what is your best guess?" Dee Dee interrupted. "We trust your opinion, Austin. You see, Destini has a daughter who is about to turn twelve years old, so we need to know something."

"If I had to guess, I would say that Ms. Wilson, with intensive chemotherapy treatments, could have as much as eight months... maybe a year. The cancer she has is quite aggressive," he said.

"How much time do I have without treatment?" Destini asked him.

"Three, maybe four months, but that's just a guess. We can't know for certain."

Without missing a beat, Destini said, as calm as could be, "There will be no treatments."

"Are you sure about that?" the doctor asked with a befuddled look on his face.

"Absolutely sure," Destini told him. "If any of you

think for a minute that I'm gonna be burned up with radiation and chemo, you got another thing comin'. I ain't goin' through that. No, sir-ree. I plan to spend the days I have left with my loved ones. If the pain gets bad enough, you can order somethin' for me. Old Dr. Campbell's grandson back home in Seraph Springs will give it to me at our little hospital there."

"As you wish," the doctor told her, again back to showing absolutely no emotion on his face or in his voice.

"Until then, Dee Dee, you and the girls are the only people who know I been sick and I wanna keep it that way," Destini ordered her. "Nobody else, you hear me? I'll tell the girls about this here cancer diagnosis when we get back home and I'll do it in my own way."

"What about Carl Alvin?" Dee Dee asked. "Can we tell him, too?"

"Well, I s'pose we could tell him, but you know how he gets. He's goin' cry and get all emotional. You gotta warn him that he's gotta keep it to hisself. It'll be hard for him, I know, but that's the way I want it."

"Hard for him? Oh, honey, my heart is breaking for you right now... and for Bunnye... and for all of us," Dee Dee cried, and she squeezed Destini's hand even harder.

"Well, it's in God's hands, as it always is," Destini said, trying extremely hard not to break down in tears. "I always pray that the heavenly Father will be merciful to me, and I thank him for his mercy, love and grace, and for forgiveness. I never forget forgiveness. Some people forget about forgiveness. That's an important one," Destini rambled on.

Dr. Tucker sat staring at her chart and then he looked up at Destini with that same blank expression on his face.

"I want to make absolutely certain that I understand your wishes, Ms. Wilson," he interrupted the two women. "You are opting for no treatment of any kind, except for pain management later on, correct?"

"Yes, sir," Destini said. "I want to be very clear with you, as well, that I don't want you to bring this up again, and I don't want any member of your staff trying to sway me to do somethin' else, other than what I just told you. I'm not goin' do it. I respect you, Dr. Tucker, and I do thank you, but whether God gives me four months or forty more years... and none of us know... I intend on living my life and not burdenin' folks with all this sickness and all this runnin' back and forth to the hospital for this, that and the other. I won't be a burden to a soul," she adamantly declared.

"Begging your pardon, Ms. Wilson, but I hardly think you will be a burden to anyone," he told her, and he came around the desk, opened his arms, and hugged her when she stood up. "I have never met a braver person, or one that was more positive or caring. I completely understand. Please know that my staff and I will work hard to ensure that your wishes are abided by."

"May I kiss you on the cheek?" Destini asked him.

"You are such a kind man."

The doctor grinned, and then he said, "You can, but I am going to kiss you on the cheek first." And so he did, and the two shared another hug.

"Well, Dee Dee, let me get my face and myself together, and then we'll go," Destini said, as she let go of the doctor. "What do you think is the best time to talk to the girls and Carl Alvin?"

"Honey, I don't think we should hold off," Dee Dee said, with her voice beginning to crack a little. "Let's phone them now and have them meet us at the camp, okay? We should be there in about an hour or so. I'll tell them to make a light lunch for us, and then afterward we can tell them about… you know… about this situation. Is that good?"

"That's perfect," Destini said, barely above a whisper. "Just perfect."

Chapter 21

The drive back to Seraph Springs for Dee Dee and Destini was odd and a bit uncomfortable, to say the least, with the proverbial elephant in the room taking up a lot of space in Dee Dee's plush, oversized SUV. However, it seemed to be a given that what just played out in the doctor's office would not be talked about until Destini was darned good and ready. For that, Destini was truly thankful.

Instead, the two women chatted about simple, everyday things, and then they listened to some music. They even sang along with the likes of Aretha Franklin and Otis Redding, whose songs played on the outrageous sound system in Dee Dee's car.

"It's almost like being at a concert!" Destini shouted above the music.

"I know!" Dee Dee shouted back. "Except one of 'em's dead and the other one is close to it!"

Destini's heart sunk into the pit of her stomach at that declaration, although, she knew Dee Dee meant nothing by it, other than she was referring to the two musical artists. It was simply an innocent statement, she knew, since Dee Dee just kept on singing along with the music. As for Destini, it abruptly brought back Mama Tee's words when she interpreted the dream about the deer and the ducks. For now, though, she needed to shake off all those dreaded thoughts and feelings and go back to singing along with Dee Dee and the stereo.

Even though the two were laughing, smiling, cracking jokes, and carrying on mindless pleasantries on the ride back home, Destini could tell that Dee Dee was dying inside and weeping buckets of invisible tears, because, quite frankly, she was, too. Except that she was also praying and wondering and hoping for some sort of miracle. No one would have guessed, though, what was really going on inside Destini's mind because she was good at covering up emotions. Almost as good as Dee Dee.

"No one in the outside world can see what's going on in someone's heart," Destini thought. "Only God can see that... only God."

About halfway home, Dee Dee turned the music off and Destini immediately began to hum a beautiful melody.

"What is that song you're humming?" Dee Dee asked her. "I believe I listened to Mama Tee sing that same song when I was younger."

"Oh, yes, it's an old song," Destini said. "It's called "Be Not Afraid".

"Oh, Destini, please sing some of it for me, will you?" Dee Dee pleaded with her. "I'd really like to hear it again."

Without further ado, and with her voice as clear as a crystal bell, Destini obliged.

"Oh, oh, Peter, be not afraid,
Jesus said, Oh, Peter, Peter, be not afraid,
Oh, Peter, be not afraid.

Walk out on the water, be not afraid,
Peter, you denied me, be not afraid,
Jesus said, Peter, you denied me, be not afraid.

Peter you denied me, be not afraid,
Walk out on the water, be not afraid.

I am Mary's baby, Peter, be not afraid,
Oh, I am Mary's baby, be not afraid,
I am Mary's baby, be not afraid.

Walk out on the water,
Walk out on the water,
Walk out on the water,
Be not afraid."

Dee Dee sang along with Destini toward the end of the song, but then she choked up on the last verse.

"Don't you start bawling on me now," Destini warned her.

"Who's bawling?" Dee Dee challenged her. "There better not be anyone crying in this car. It will ruin my beautiful upholstery. No, ma'am... ain't nobody doin' no cryin'."

Destini knew her cousin was lying through her

teeth, but that's why she loved her so much. She needed someone strong like Dee Dee to help her get through this time of pain and anguish.

As Dee Dee pulled off the main highway and onto the dirt road leading to Camp EZ, Destini gave her another warning.

"Let me do the telling, you hear me? I mean it," she added. "The only reason I say that is because I know you, Dee Dee. I know you like the back of my hand. You're the kindest person in the world, but when you get excited, you do prattle on sometimes. I say that with love, girl. I can say stuff like that to you. Nobody else outside the family can, but I sure can."

"Yes, and you do," Dee Dee agreed, but she smiled at her, letting her know she wasn't offended.

Nadine, Wanda Faye and Carl Alvin had come out onto the porch when they saw Dee Dee's car coming down the drive. The collective look of fear on their faces could not betray what they were feeling. Destini knew everyone was nervous, apprehensive and concerned. So was she, but she knew what she had to do. After inhaling a deep, cleansing breath and then slowly letting it out, she pasted a smile on her face.

"Whew!" she exclaimed, as she and Dee Dee stepped up onto the porch. "That sun is shining so pretty today, isn't it? It's not too cool out here, either. Let's just sit here on the porch for a minute before we go inside, okay? Nadine, honey, would you please get me a glass of ice water?"

"Sure, honey," Nadine said, and then she glanced

over at Wanda Faye with a questioning look in her eyes.

It was highly unusual for Destini to request anything from anyone, as far as bringing her something to eat or drink, or doing anything for her, and it seemed the girls weren't prepared for it.

"You know what? Let's all have some water or a cup of coffee, maybe even a mixed drink… whatever y'all want. In fact, I'll help y'all go get it," Destini said, and she started for the door.

"No, ma'am, you won't," Wanda Faye told her. "You stay right here on this porch and have a seat. Me and Nadine will be right back."

"Okay," Destini said, and she sat down on one of the old rockers that lined the length of the porch.

When they came back, Nadine handed Destini a glass of ice water and a linen napkin, while Wanda Faye poured some freshly brewed, ice cold sweet tea for everyone else. Nadine opted for a cup of coffee.

"Thank you, Nadine," Destini said. "Thank you. I appreciate it."

"Sure thing, honey," Nadine said with a nervous chuckle, and then she sat down in the chair next to her. "You know, Destini, Christmas is just around the corner and I want to be on the "nice" list, not the "naughty" one."

Everyone had a good laugh and then it went quiet for a few moments. The tension in the air was thick as mud.

"What's on your mind, Destini?" Nadine asked, in an attempt to break the unnerving silence.

"Well, since you asked..." Destini began. "Y'all remember when we were little girls, and in the summertime it would be so hot that Mama Tee and Miss Jewell would make us lie down after lunch? Then, they would talk about all sorts o' things when they was cannin' or bakin' or even prayin'?"

All the girls nodded their heads and then Destini continued.

"Remember how we hated that, but as we lied on those old beds and sometimes on those hard pallets, we would whisper and tell each other our deepest, darkest secrets? Then, we'd do the pinkie promise? Y'all remember that?"

"I remember those times like it was yesterday," Wanda Faye said. "We'd all lock our pinkie fingers together and swear we wouldn't tell a soul any of our secrets."

"Lord, yes!" Nadine piped up. "I also remember those times Dee Dee was there and she'd bring us the big news from Turpricone."

"Oh, yeah," Dee Dee said. "Those were the days."

"I remember at the time we thought a lot of it was such racy news about some of the folks in town, like Miss So and So's hair ain't really that color. She gets it from a bottle," Nadine said. "Or so and so's daddy spends more time at his secretary's house than he does at home. Or so and so's brother is the handsomest thing, and wouldn't we love to smooch on him."

The girls all laughed and so did Carl Alvin.

"Sometimes, I'd be in the other room, but I'd crawl

up to the door where I knew y'all were… not resting, by the way, and I'd listen to all your dark secrets and laugh myself silly," he said.

"Why, you little scoundrel!" Destini shouted, and then it grew quiet again.

After a few awkward, silent moments passed, Destini continued.

"I want all of y'all to pretend we're at Mama Tee's right now, lying down on them pallets," she said. "Close your eyes, and think back. Go on, now. All of y'all, close your eyes."

After checking to make sure everyone had their eyes closed, Destini went on to tell them a story.

"Now, think about how we were then; little girls… happy and hopeful… and we still happy and hopeful today," she said, and then she paused for a second. "I got a story I'm goin' tell y'all. Remember the stories y'all would beg me to tell? Keep your eyes closed now."

Again, Destini checked to make sure all eyes were closed, and they were.

"They was a little girl born outside a small town in a house on a farm not far from the Suwannee River. She grew up with four of the best friends she could ever have, and all of 'em looked different than her, but it didn't matter to her or them, because they were bound by something stronger and more powerful than this world could ever give or offer. They were bound by the unbreakable bonds of pure, unconditional love and acceptance. They never talked about it. They never expressed it, but in their hearts, they knew. They were all rocked in that big ol' rocker on Mama Tee's front porch. They were held in her ample lap and hummed to on hot spring and summer afternoons. They was rocked when they thought their hearts would break over some awful thing that happened. They all knew laughter, though, and mischief, good food, going to church, telling secrets, and most of all, helping each other. They knew about love. They just never talked much about it."

Destini paused to take a sip of her water and then she continued.

"That unspoken love gave them the hope they needed to move on with their lives," she said. "One day, the man, as the old black folks would say, or the Cap'n, as others called him, or just plain ol' Mr. Hamp Brayerford… well, he was the head man in the white community and he told this little black girl that he needed her to help out at Camp EZ, and so she went. Over time, their feelings for each other turned into something and from that came my precious Bunnye. All of y'all in your hearts suspected at the time, but you didn't' say a word, not a mumbling word."

Destini was beginning to get nervous now because this happy story she was weaving was about to have an extremely unhappy ending, but she knew she had to press on, no matter how difficult it was.

"So, my precious baby came," Destini continued. "I kept on working, though, and the man, the Cap'n soon got older. Then, one day he fell ill, and not long afterward he left me… never to come back. He left me with our child, a heart full of love, and more money and land than could be used in ten lifetimes. He did all that for me and his child. He didn't care what folks would say. He loved us. I didn't care what folks said about any of y'all, either, and you didn't care what they said about me. We all gave 'em plenty to talk about, though, didn't we?"

The whole group gently laughed at this and nodded, but all their eyes stayed shut.

"One day, the little black girl, who's now a big lady, began to feel kinda poorly. She called her cousin and said maybe I need to see a doctor. So, she took me, and I have seen the doctor… a good looking white man he was. He told me I was not a well woman. Less than six months to live, according to that good lookin' white man, but you know what? His last name is spelled T-U-C-K-E-R and not G-O-D."

Now, a plethora of lips were trembling on the front porch of Camp EZ and tears were freely flowing down reddened cheeks. Destini could hear the sobbing and it made her heart ache even more, but she stood firm and tenacious, unwilling to give in to defeat. Not yet, anyway.

"Now, I want all y'all to join pinkies with me and swear… swear to me, swear," she ordered everyone, and they all nodded their heads in agreement. "We's all on that pallet now. So, swear with all that's holy. This story I just told y'all stays on this porch until I say differently."

Everyone reached out their hands, shaking and

trembling as they were, and clasped pinkies together with Destini, who made them repeat the age-old promise.

"I swear with all that is in my heart, and to the Father, the Son and the Holy Ghost, that this story I just told y'all is to be kept secret."

Each word was uttered by everyone in a solemn, heartbreaking tone, as more tears flowed. The only one not shedding tears was Destini. She was as calm as the deep blue sea.

"God will send a vision," Destini said. "I am praying for it, and he never fails me. Even if he takes me home, he has not failed me. Now y'all dry up," she added. "Remember your promise. Go wash your faces, and let's eat lunch. I'm starved. Nadine, I hope we got more than tuna fish salad and canned peaches."

At this, Nadine and Wanda Faye laughed out loud, and Dee Dee spit her iced tea halfway across the porch.

"Dear God," Dee Dee said, laughing. "All of us are a bunch of fattening hogs, wondering what we're going to eat after hearing that heartbreaking story, but it's important. So… what have we got, ladies?" she asked.

"Well…" Nadine began. "Let me tell y'all something. You see, we know you pretty good, if you haven't figured that out already, so early this morning we had Louie and Dink in the river… in a safe part of the river, that is."

"Oh, Lord, no!" Destini screeched, as her eyes lit up.

"Yes, ma'am," Nadine said. "Suwannee River

catfish, grits, hushpuppies, guava or mayhaw jelly, cane syrup, if you want it, and for dessert, some of the best lemon meringue pie you'll ever wrap your lips around, honey."

Everyone applauded, more out of nervous tension than anything else, and then they went inside and sat down around the dining room table. Destini asked everyone to join hands.

"Say a blessing for us, Carl Alvin," she said.

Knowing how Carl Alvin was given to emotion most of the time, when the occasion called for it, that is, he surprised Destini and everyone else, and even made them laugh.

"Dear Lord, add your blessings to these delectable victuals," he prayed. "May they add to thy glory and not to our middles. Amen."

"Amen!" Destini shouted. "Short and sweet. Just how I like it. Brother Ben shot duh roostuh and killed duh hen. Let's eat!"

And they did, all of them, voraciously, and with a fellowship among them of trusted old friends.

While they ate, they talked about Miss Sissy and her young man in New Orleans. They talked about the whippings Miss Jewell would give them for whispering and cutting up in the House of Prayer. They laughed and talked about slipping off to the old smokehouse behind Mama Tee's house to smoke cigarettes, and how Mr. Hamp and Mama Tee had caught them and made them smoke cigarette after cigarette until they were green in the face, hoping they would never want another one.

"The only ones who didn't get sick were Nadine and Wanda Faye," Carl Alvin said.

Wanda Faye laughed and said, "We had more experience smoking than y'all. We used to sneak them from Daddy's cigarette packs and we were smoking a good, long while before any of y'all started."

They talked about slipping off to the river and how Dee Dee fell in one day, and they thought she was going to drown, and how Carl Alvin pulled her to the bank. They talked about how they tried to explain her wet clothes and wet hair to Mama Tee, who was having none of it, and who made them all take a nap. Then, she and Mr. Hamp gave them a stern talking to about the dangers of the river.

They talked about school days, and they talked about the upcoming days of the holidays, and of Dee Dee's wedding next year to Ricardo. It was then that Dee Dee quietly told them she was going to the little girl's room. Nadine followed her there and then Wanda Faye joined her out in the hallway.

From behind the closed door, Nadine and Wanda Faye could hear both the sink and the shower faucets running full blast, and the toilet kept flushing again and again. They heard the pounding on the floor and Dee Dee's muffled screams into a towel. Here was the heiress to one of the greatest fortunes in the county having a breakdown inside the bathroom, afraid to let anyone see her so distraught.

"Do you think we ought to go in?" Wanda Faye

askcd Nadine.

"No, honey, and besides, you know she's got the door locked," Nadine said. "She's got to cry it out. She's got to scream it out all by herself. She won't do it in front of anyone, but she has to do it. Let her be until she comes out. You know Dee Dee. She'll make up some story about the candles or the pine wood or something in this cabin that's causing her eyes to be all red and puffy. You'll never see her break down in front of any of us. It's the way she's made. It's just Dee Dee."

"Okay, well, let's get back to the others before they come looking for us," Wanda Faye suggested.

A short while later, Dee Dee emerged from the bathroom. She did a fairly good job of covering up her grief, as well as her swollen eyes, for the most part, that is. Meanwhile, lunch was over and Nadine and Wanda Faye were clearing the table.

"Dee Dee, I want to ask you something, sugar," Destini said, after Dee Dee sat back down at the table.

"Ask away," she said.

"I want you to play something on the piano for me, and I want all of us to sing."

"Ahh… I think I know what you're looking for, Destini," Dee Dee said, seeming back to her old self again. "Come on, everyone. Gather around the piano, if you will."

Dee Dee struck a familiar chord on the keys with her long, slender fingers and the whole group sang one of Destini's favorite Christmas carols, "The First

Noel", followed by several more, even though it was a bit early to be singing about Christmas. When they finished about half an hour later, there was a different look on the faces of everyone in the room, especially on Destini's face.

"Now, we can move on," Destini said, solemnly, but succinctly. "Let's not mention this again, unless I bring it up," she added, as she looked into the eyes of all her dear friends.

Everyone agreed, and to Destini, it seemed they all had more joy in their hearts now, whether it was her imagination thinking so, or just her hope that her friends would be better able to cope with her uncertain future.

Chapter 22

Dee Dee's inner turmoil

Later that evening, Dee Dee drove her black Range Rover over to her Aunt Hattie's house in Turpricone. At least, that's where she was originally headed when she left Camp EZ. All the while she was driving, she kept praying and praying, and trying to make sense out of things, until the only thing she could come up with was an ear-piercing scream, "Why?!"

Being alone in the car, she let the tears fall freely and each one stung worse than the ones before.

"Why?!" she screamed again. "Why is this happening to Destini?! It's not fair! It's just not fair! She's too young!"

Her head was throbbing. It felt like one of those sick headaches one has when they're stressed out to the max. She reached into the console beside her and grabbed a single package of powdered Knock Out, one of the best headache powders ever invented. It was good for hangovers, headaches, you name it. Knock Out powders had never let her down before and she needed it to do its magic now more than ever. After washing it down with some bottled water, she turned on the stereo and searched until she found something soft, slow and soothing.

She had known Destini Wilson since the two of them were mere toddlers. They had grown up together between Mama Tee's house, her Uncle Hamp's cabin, and an odd assortment of places in and around the town of Seraph Springs. Destini's life had been so intertwined with hers that Dee Dee could practically predict the next words in any story Destini shared, which she did numerous times. It always drove Destini crazy, she knew, to think that someone could know her so well. Dee Dee also had that same connection with Nadine, Wanda Faye and even Carl Alvin for that matter. It was uncanny, to say the least.

The four girls had been an odd quartet of children, tagging along with each other as they traveled to so many different places around town and elsewhere, but it worked for them. Throughout Wanda Faye's unfortunate first marriage to Chester Easley, on to her still successful marriage to Dink, then through all of Nadine's life adventures, and all the children everyone bore, as well as Destini's roller coaster ride of a life, which seemed to affect everyone else like a roller coaster, too, all except Dee Dee, that is… but through it all, they had stuck together like Super Glue.

As the Knock Out powder started to take effect, Dee Dee's pounding headache seemed to let up just a bit.

"Thank you, Knock Out," she muttered, as she rubbed her temples, which was hard to do while driving, but she took turns alternating hands on the steering wheel.

Soon, her thoughts began to wander away from Destini's plight, and she focused on her fiancé, Ricardo, for a moment.

"I need to talk to you, baby," she thought. "I need to do it now, too."

She hit the speed dial on her phone and made certain she had the Bluetooth turned on, so she could hear him through the car's speakers. He answered on the second ring.

"Dee Dee!" Ricardo shouted, sounding extremely chipper during such a somber moment. "How are you, my darling?" he asked her.

She couldn't even answer him. She just started sobbing uncontrollably, which was something she never did, but she couldn't seem to stop herself. She erroneously thought she had accomplished her emotional purge in the bathroom at Camp EZ, but there was evidently still much more grief dammed up inside of her.

"What's wrong?" he asked her. "What is wrong, my darling?" he repeated, in a voice so soothing it was almost God-like, she thought.

When she finally caught her breath, she said in a distraught tone that was interrupted by sobs and sniffles, "It's De... Des... Destini."

"What's wrong with our beautiful Destini?" he asked, still calm as a cucumber.

"She has cancer, Ricardo, and it's terminal," she managed to say, and then her voice returned to a halfway normal tone. "She's taking it well, though. I thought I could handle it, but I can't. I cannot bear this alone, honey. I know it's a lot to ask, but may I come to you? Or can you come to me? I truly need you right now. I need to talk to you and tell you all about it. I need to feel your arms around me, baby."

"Think no more about it," he valiantly told her. "I am fifteen minutes from the airport and my business here is all wrapped up. Our company pilot is with me, too. I shall be by your side in about two hours... maybe a little more. Just hold on, my beautiful Dee Dee."

"Oh, sweetheart, thank you. Thank you so much," she cried. "I'll meet you at the airport," she said.

As soon as she ended the call, she made a U-turn and headed back east to catch the interstate over to Jacksonville. She met him at the airport a couple hours later, just as his plane landed. Then, she drove him back to her late Uncle Hamp's hideaway cabin in Seraph Springs where she poured out her heart to him, as she had never poured it out before.

She related to him as many heartwarming stories of her childhood with Destini as she could remember, each one more precious than the others. She told him of the many challenges that Destini, as well as the girls and Carl Alvin had faced over the years, and how they had all triumphed over each hurdle.

All the while they sat together on the front porch swing, he held her close to him and never once interrupted her. He merely sat quietly and listened to her every word.

When she was finished, he went inside the cabin and made a phone call. When he came back out, he took her by the hand and said he wanted to take her out for a bite to eat.

"I don't know about you, but I'm starving," he told her. "Give me the keys, honey. I'll drive."

He took her to a quaint little restaurant on the river near Pittstown. Dee Dee didn't realize it, but she, too, was famished. She wound up ordering a rare T-bone steak and ate the whole thing, down to the juicy bone. Ricardo had the catfish, his favorite meal, he told her.

As they ate, they talked about inconsequential things at Dee Dee's insistence. Then, their evening meal was topped off with Arlene's famous pecan pie for dessert, along with coffee that was piping hot and restorative.

As they were about to leave the restaurant, Ricardo made an announcement that nearly knocked her off her chair.

"We will be married on New Year's Eve," he said, smiling from ear to ear.

"What did you say?" she asked, wide-eyed and clearly stunned.

"We will be married on New Year's Eve," he repeated. "Don't you think that would be best?"

Dee Dee stood up, walked around to the other side of the table, and gently pulled Ricardo up out of his seat. Right there, in a public place, before God and everyone else who was in the restaurant, she shouted,

"I do!"

If she ever doubted that she had made the right choice for a life partner, all those doubts were gone now. She would be married to Ricardo on New Year's Eve at Camp EZ, and the rest would take care of itself. She wasn't thinking beyond that point right now. She took his hand in hers and they walked into their future.

Chapter 23

News in any small town always travels as quick as a lightning bolt on a balmy summer's eve, and Seraph Springs was no exception. There was always one person you couldn't hide the truth from and that was Mama Tee. She immediately sensed something was wrong when Destini came to her house today and she made sure her beloved granddaughter knew it.

Destini had been dreading the visit ever since she found out about her illness, but she knew she had to tell Mama Tee before someone else slipped up and let the cat out of the bag. When she reached down to kiss her grandmother, Mama Tee drew back as if to look at her... could she see, that is.

"You ain't yourself, girl!" Mama Tee barked at her.

"What are you talkin' about?" Destini retorted.

The uncharacteristic, gentle lilt of her voice, however, gave her away and it was all Mama Tee needed to know. Her child had trouble and she could hear it in her voice. It was a voice she knew all too well.

Mama Tee had told her many times that a mother or grandmother who is truly connected to a child has that sixth sense and instinctively knows when trouble is brewing, or when they have joyous news to share.

"It comes across clear as a bell," Mama Tee had

told her. "They hear it in their voices. Just as I know how many steps it is from the front porch to my recliner, and how many steps from that recliner to the bathroom, and what time Estella will be here to give me my daily insulin and check my blood sugar."

Estella Brown was Mama Tee's cherished, long time neighbor and distant cousin, who used to work as a nurse for Dr. Campbell until her retirement two years ago.

"I know what time you come to bring me my breakfast and lunch, and my dinner, unless Dee Dee or one of the girls brings it, and they always call before they come over," Mama Tee went on. "Somethin' is wrong wid you, Destini, and you better go ahead and tell me, girl. I ain't so old I cain't tear yer behind up. It's somethin' and somethin' big. I can hear it. I feels it in my bones. You best be tellin' me, girl. I wanna know the whole truth, too."

If there was one person in the world… in this world… to whom Destini could never lie, it was the old woman sitting in front of her right now. She knew that for a fact, and so she told her everything. Then, she cried and she cried, and in between the crying Mama Tee held her hand.

When she finished, Mama Tee said as calmly as the midnight sea, "What man thinks and what God has in store is two different things."

"What did you say?" Destini asked, as she choked back her tears.

"I *said*," Mama Tee began with emphasis, as she

clenched her teeth together. "What man thinks and what God has in store is two different things."

"I don't understand. What are you saying?" Destini asked, knowing there were always double meanings behind many things that would come out of Mama Tee's mouth.

"I said what I said, and I know what I know," Mama Tee told her, and she left it at that.

Destini looked at her grandmother and not one tear came from her blinded eyes; not one expression was on her face, either, save that of contentment.

Later that night, after baring her soul to Mama Tee, Destini drove back to Camp EZ and went to bed. For the first time in several days, she slept. She slept soundly, too, until the sun rose in the sky the next morning.

Chapter 24

Thanksgiving, which was normally the biggest event of the year at Camp EZ, came and went quickly, but it just wasn't the same this year as in years past. Oh, everyone put on a happy face and there was more food to eat than you could shake a stick at, but the atmosphere was much quieter than usual, especially since Phil Jr. and all his crew had left the previous day, so they could spend the holiday with their families.

Destini could feel the uneasiness throughout the day and couldn't shake it, no matter how hard she tried. The bravery she'd been displaying to family and friends about her illness was on its last threads and she didn't know how much longer she could pretend that she wasn't afraid. The looks of pity she was getting from certain people in her inner circle were enough to make her want to scream. She was also dreading the day she would have to break the news to her daughter.

It was like a somber pallor was hanging over Camp EZ all day long, perhaps in comparison to how a stubborn calf might feel on its way to the slaughterhouse, Destini thought, as she wallowed in her own sadness.

Even Little Hamp's Thanksgiving birthday celebration was less than the stellar event it should have been, because the young two-year-old had come down with a cold. His mother, Wanda Faye, kept apologizing for his cranky behavior.

"Good grief," she had mumbled to Destini in frustration, as she tried to get Little Hamp to stop crying. "What good is this nursing degree I have if I can't even make my own baby feel better?"

She finally had to take the little guy home and put him to bed with some medication to clear up his congestion, thus missing out on the big feast later in the evening.

Then, even though Miss Jewell and Essie had been released from the hospital the previous day, they were both still not feeling up to par, so they, too, wound up leaving the festivities earlier than usual.

The Sunday following the big Thanksgiving feast fell on the next to the last day in November. At Mt. Nebo, a special meeting of prayer and thanksgiving in anticipation of the Christmas season and the end of the year was called, but it turned into much more than that.

Sister Violet Jackson, who was the chairman of the church usher board and one of Mama Tee's closest confidantes, knew enough from talking to Mama Tee that she sensed in her bones something was just not right in the family fold. The word went out from the pastor of the church to the District superintendent, and right on up to the Bishop.

Mt. Nebo was overflowing at the seams that Sunday, as the pastor called the faithful to the altar to pray. As each word left the pastor's lips, the entire congregation, along with the forty-member choir standing behind him in their gold-trimmed, white robes, sang the words to "A Charge To Keep I Have, A Soul To Sanctify."

It was a low, almost primitive, but melodic moan as they sang; the moan… it was an utterance which the Lord understands and feels in the souls of his faithful when words belie what is on their hearts.

After the song, the pastor thanked God for all his many blessings, for his mercy, grace, and love, and for forgiveness. He thanked him for waking him up that morning. He thanked him for making a way for him when there seemed to be no way. He thanked him for watching over him and the flock at Mt. Nebo, and all God's children, and he thanked him for the wonderful privilege of prayer.

As he prayed, a member of the church stood beside him, fanning him and wiping perspiration from his forehead.

The congregation responded with, "Amen! Thank you, Jesus! Hallelujah, and thank you, sir!"

The entire congregation got caught up in the spirit of the prayer and began to hum very low, but audibly, as the prayer was coming to an end. The choir then picked it up, as the piano player struck the ivory keys.

"Oh, oh, I know I've been changed.
Oh, oh, I know I've been changed.
Oh, oh, I know I've been changed.
The angels in heaven done signed my name.

The angels in heaven done signed my name."

They sang with abandon, they sang with their souls magnifying the secrets of their souls. They sang from the depths of their beings. They sang with everything that was inside them.

The bishop's assistant, who had driven all the way from Miami for the service, was caught up in the spirit of the song and the spirit of the people. When he went to the podium, he stated that never in his many years of experience in service to the Lord had he witnessed such fervor in the spirit.

Among those standing in the choir was Destini, who broke into the solo part of the song without prodding, and all eyes turned toward her.

Destini sang:
    "Lord I went up on the mountain to pray."
The choir responded:
    "The angels in heaven done signed my name."
Destini sang:
    "My soul got happy and I stayed all day,
    The angels in heaven done signed my name.
    The waters of Jordan are chilly and cold
    The angels in heaven done signed my name.
    They chill the body, but not the soul,
    The angels in heaven done signed my name.
And then the choir came in:
    "Oh, oh, I know I've been changed,
    Oh, I know I've been changed,

Oh, oh, I know I've been changed,
The angels in heaven done signed my name,
The angels in heaven done signed my name."

Suddenly, Destini fell at the altar, slain in the spirit, and the women fanned her, standing around her like a shield. She felt something within her move, and inside her head she heard Mama Tee's words; "What man thinks and what God has in store is two different things."

The words seemed to shout in her head. She came up from the altar and held up her hand, and there, before the body of Christ that had always boosted her in her weariness, celebrated her successes, been there for her on any occasion, she testified to what God had done for her.

In her mind and in her heart she knew what had just happened. She knew it from the bottom of her soul. No one had to tell her otherwise.

Later that afternoon, Dee Dee stopped by Camp EZ to check on Destini and was surprised to see her looking so well. Destini asked her if she would phone the doctor's office in Jacksonville and ask for an appointment for testing at the hospital; the same tests she was given that pronounced her death sentence a few short weeks ago.

"Well, I'm not sure why you want to do this, but I'll call them tomorrow," Dee Dee told her. "Oh, and don't worry, I will be more than happy to drive you there and back."

The next morning, Dee Dee made the call and she was able to get Destini worked in the following day for the testing and the reading of the tests would be within forty-eight hours. It seems a friend of hers from the huge department store where she worked as a buyer was married to one of the hospital administrators, she explained to Destini.

"Girl, is there any connection you don't have?" Destini asked her when she phoned her to tell her about the appointments.

"Nope, not too many," Dee Dee said, laughing. "I'll pick you up tomorrow around eight in the morning, okay? Then, we can go back on Friday to get the results."

"Thank you, Dee Dee," Destini said. "I don't know what I would do without you."

"Well, let's hope you never have to find out," Dee Dee told her.

The next day, the doctors ran the same battery of tests at Destini's request. Dr. Tucker told Dee Dee that he hated to see Destini go through the tests again, but he reluctantly complied, not knowing her reason for doing so.

What was really unexpected were the test results two days later. When Dr. Tucker walked into the examination room where Destini and Dee Dee were anxiously waiting, he looked stunned and was shaking his head, but smiling at the same time.

After the words came out of his mouth, Dee Dee's raucous scream and Destini's ear-piercing hallelujah could be heard throughout the corridors of the entire doctor's building. Even people standing outside the office along the street heard the emotion-packed declarations of joy and triumph coming from inside.

Meanwhile, back in Seraph Springs, Wanda Faye was bringing Mama Tee her lunch when the old woman suddenly grabbed her arm.

"Let up and gone now!" Mama Tee yelled.

"What did you say?" Wanda Faye asked her.

"Let up and gone away from Destini!" she yelled again.

"Mama Tee, you're not making any sense," Wanda Faye told her.

Just then, Wanda Faye's cell phone rang and she answered it.

"Wanda Faye, this is Dee Dee. Put me on speaker so that Mama Tee can hear," Dee Dee ordered her, and so she did. "We're all in a conference call now, Wanda Faye. I've got Carl Alvin on the line with us, as well as Nadine. Are you there, Mama Tee?" Dee Dee asked.

"I'm here, chil'," the old woman said, smiling.

"Well, there's something you all need to know, so I'm putting Destini on now," Dee Dee said.

"Hi, y'all!" Destini shouted. "God healed me! You hear that? God done healed me! I'm goin' be with y'all for a while longer!"

Mama Tee, who seldom displayed any emotion, shook in her chair and shouted, "Glory, glory, glory to God! Thank you, oh, thank you, suh! Thank you! Thank you! Amen!"

Mama Tee continued shaking, as if she had just been poked with an electric cattle prod. It lasted for about ten seconds and then she settled back in her chair and started to hum a song. It was that same age old spiritual they sang in church last Sunday.

"Ohh, yes, Mama Tee," Destini cried, as her eyes filled with tears. "The angels in heaven done signed my name!"

Dee Dee's next phone call was to Ricardo, who was down in Miami on business again. Even though the urgency to get married right away had passed, with Destini seemingly out of the woods, they both agreed that they still wanted to get married on New Year's Eve, as they had discussed earlier.

"The wedding will go on," Ricardo told her.

"Oh, thank you, Ricardo," Dee Dee said. "I love you so much."

Chapter 25

By the time Christmas Eve rolled around, the mood at Camp EZ had brightened exponentially. There were so many things to be thankful for and even more things to celebrate. The place looked utterly magnificent with all the Christmas decorations, both inside and outdoors.

The annual brunch was a barn-burner, fun-filled time with holiday merry-makers enjoying the caroling, the socializing, the mule and horse drawn wagon rides, and, as always, plentiful good food and drinks.

The big twelve-foot Christmas tree in the great room was lavishly adorned with all the decorations made by the late Jerri Faye Linton and Miss Jewell's Bible Drill group. The red velvet bows, which were Mr. Hamp's favorite, were utilized exclusively. The other two trees that the kids had decorated out on the porch had seemed to shrink amid all the extra ornaments the kids kept adding, but they were still unique and beautiful in their own right.

There was a slight change in the tradition this year, however. Destini, at the request of Mama Tee, had booked a professional photographer from Pittstown to come on Christmas Day to shoot photographs.

"I wants everybody to wear a Santy Claus hat

tomorrow, and I want everyone of y'all to be smilin' for the picture and wearin' whatever y'all feel most comfortable wearin'," Mama Tee ordered everyone.

About nine o'clock on Christmas morning, the entire group assembled, including Dee Dee's Aunt Hattie and Aunt Nanny, who were both wearing beautiful, matching burgundy sweaters and winter white slacks.

"No Christmas themed sweaters for us this year," Aunt Hattie announced when the two of them arrived. "This year we're more reserved, isn't that right, Nanny?"

"Yes, more reserved," Nanny replied with a stiff upper lip.

"Well, you both look fabulous," Nadine told the two women.

Others, though, did wear Christmas-themed sweaters, one of whom was Dee Dee, wearing a red and white sweater emblazoned with a huge, green Christmas tree that would light up in a rainbow of colors.

Her Aunt Hattie just shook her head and mumbled, "My Lord. All that money spent on charm school and on her education and look at that, would you, Nanny?"

Nanny didn't know what to say, evidently, because her eyes lit up and she giggled, as if she thought Dee Dee's sweater was the coolest thing she had ever seen.

Others in the group were more low-key and conservative, wearing jeans and flannel shirts, as it was a tad nippy outside. The only one wearing a dress was

Bunnye and she looked absolutely stunning. Destini proudly told everyone that Bunnye had made the dress herself and had stayed up past midnight putting the final touches on it.

Meanwhile, Mama Tee sported a bright red outfit with a zip up jacket and pants to match. She topped off her ensemble with a pair of sparkling gold sneakers. In her pierced ears she wore lighted Christmas bulb earrings that got the attention of all the children.

After about twenty minutes of moving this one here and that one there, the photographer finally managed to get the entire group assembled around the Christmas tree in just the right positions so he could snap the photograph. After twenty or so takes, he said he was done and everyone was relieved; no one more so than the photographer himself.

Never forgetting her manners, though, Destini invited him to partake of some food and drink. He declined the invitation, but he left with one of Miss Jewell's chocolate swirl cakes. He said he remembered purchasing one at a church fundraiser.

"I'll never forget how tasty and delicious that cake was," he complimented Miss Jewell before he left.

The celebrating continued well into the afternoon. Wrapping paper and ribbons and bows were scattered everywhere, and all the children seemed happy and content as their Christmas wish lists had been granted.

About three o'clock, Duke, Louie and Dink pulled up the Camp EZ wagons for the annual ride down to the river. Mama Tee was helped onto the first wagon, which would lead the procession.

While everyone was singing Christmas carols, Mama Tee asked Dee Dee, who was sitting beside her, if there was any of Mr. Hamp's special Christmas moonshine left.

"Funny you should ask," Dee Dee said, and out came the mason jars and the Styrofoam cups.

"Ah-hah! Pour it up!" Mama Tee shouted. "We gots to have the Christmas cheer! Let's all have a drink to Christmas, to friends and to loved ones... present and absent," she added.

Everyone in all three wagons drank their moonshine, excluding the kids, who had lemonade, and then Mama Tee led them all in one of her favorite Christmas carols, "Jingle Bells".

"Remember today, girls," Mama Tee said to Destini and Bunnye after the song finished. "Remember the good Lord above made this possible, along with that boy with the big ol' feet. Biggest feet I ever seen on a baby," she added with a loud cackle, referring to her old friend, the late Hamp Brayerford.

"Amen to that, Mama Tee," Destini said. "He did have some big ol' feet."

"Amen from me, too," Bunnye said, as she hugged her mama.

Once they all made it down to the river, everyone disembarked and then sat around in a circle on top of numerous blankets. Stories were told, songs were sung, and everyone was truly enjoying the fellowship of friends and family.

"Lord, I dread gettin' all that stuff back at the camp cleaned up for Dee Dee's weddin'," Destini said, stretching and yawning, as the late afternoon sun began its descent. "I'm about wore out."

Dee Dee happened to overhear her, and said, "Well cousin, a little change of plans here. You can leave the Christmas stuff where it is. I'm having my reception at the camp on New Year's Eve, but the wedding is going to be at Saint Mary's, the little Catholic Church over in Pittstown," she added, and she kissed Ricardo on the lips.

There was a collective gasp from everyone and a lot of startled looks, especially from Dee Dee's two aunts.

"You see, I converted to Catholicism," Dee Dee explained before anyone could protest. "I've been taking classes at the church since Ricardo and I decided to get married. I knew what it would mean to my future husband and how important it was to his family, so I converted."

"Good!" Mama Tee shouted. "You both are startin' out on the right path worshipping together. A divided house won't stand, and Dee Dee, honey, I am proud of you," she went on. "Cuban boy!" she suddenly called out. "Hey, Cuban boy! Rick! Whatever your name is… come over here and give me a hug, boy!"

Ricardo was cracking up, but he managed to come over and hug the old woman.

"Oh, you sho' do smell so nice," Mama Tee told him. "You my baby now, Ricardo. See… I knew yer darn name the whole time. I was jus' joshin' you," she added, and then she cackled like a hen, obviously amused with her humor.

Everybody started laughing. Even Ricardo's parents were wiping joyful tears from their eyes.

"Now, Mr. Ricky Ricardo, you tell your folks to come over here and give me a hug," Mama Tee ordered him. "I want a hug from both o' dem."

Mr. and Mrs. Fernandez indulged the old woman, and eagerly embraced her.

"Now, Dee Dee, you can marry, and I plan on being there," Mama Tee continued. "You better not say they ain't enough room in dat church for me."

"Mama Tee, you know you have a seat reserved for you on the front row," Dee Dee assured her.

"I'm goin' tell y'all something," Mama Tee said. "I knows enough. Each one of you ladies here, damn sho' better have some lace on your heads or a nice hat, and that includes you, Miss Hattie and Miss Nanny. I know y'all ain't that happy 'bout this baby leaving da' folds of the Methodist Church. Get over it. The Lord is the Lord, and he's happy with this chil'. Always has been."

"Point taken, Mama Tee," Hattie said. "As long as she doesn't think I'm going to do all that kneeling when they click or ring that little bell during the service."

"They ring them bells for folks to get up and down," Mama Tee told her. "Ricardo or Mama Fernandez... y'all better give us folks some hints or help us practice."

"We will be sure to clue you in," Ricardo's father

assured her. "It's really not that difficult, I promise you."

Ricardo's brother Justo added, "We won't lead you astray. We cannot. We are all in the same wagon."

"Amen," Destini said. "Speakin' o' wagons, we best be gettin' back to the camp. It's gettin' pretty dark out," she added.

The ride back to the camp was even more joyous, especially since the moonshine kept flowing from the mason jars. Everyone enjoyed themselves late into the evening, as they sat in front of a roaring fire in the great room. All the talk was centered around Dee Dee and Ricardo's wedding and all the preparations that needed doing for the reception.

"Mama, I think this is one of the best Christmases ever," Bunnye said to Destini later that night as she prepared for bed. "Thank you so much for all my presents. I love you."

"Oh, baby, I love you, too. I love you so, so much. Now, you have nothin' but sweet, sweet dreams tonight."

"I will, Mama," Bunnye said. "Goodnight."

"Goodnight, my precious baby," Destini said, and she turned out the light.

Chapter 26

Wedding plans shifted into overdrive the following day, as Anna Mary, always the meticulous planner, left no stone unturned in regards to Dee Dee and Ricardo's special day.

Anna Mary and Stanley had brought young Mary Selena with them and just as Destini had promised her back in New Orleans, Mary Selena got to spend a few days at Camp EZ with her and Bunnye. Destini, for one, was more than thrilled, especially when she saw how well the two young girls got along.

The rehearsal dinner for the wedding party was held at Dee Dee's Aunt Hattie's home the night before the wedding. It was a sit-down dinner for about a hundred people. Needless to say, Stanley was relieved that he and Anna Mary didn't have to throw a big party for Dee Dee, although, Dee Dee told him she might be asking him to throw a post-wedding shindig for the happy couple after they returned from their honeymoon.

"Hrmphh," Stanley mumbled. "We'll have to see about that."

"Yes, we will," Dee Dee said, always seeming to take such pleasure in taunting the man.

Hattie, meanwhile, had worked extremely hard with

her caterer, Daphne Gerald. The two of them had created a menu that perfectly blended the two different cultures of Florida; Anglo and Cuban. The food had everyone raving about how delicious it was.

After dinner, everyone was invited out onto the terrace to enjoy a fireworks show. It was there on the terrace that Aunt Hattie truly surprised everyone. She had engaged several members of the Jacksonville Symphony Orchestra to play "God Bless America", "The National Anthem", and the Pre-Revolutionary Cuban National Anthem, "La Bayamesa".

The Fernandez family was deeply touched by Hattie's deference to their culture, not only with the Cuban food, but now the playing of their old national anthem. They sang the lyrics with fervor and much emotion, as Dee Dee fought back tears of joy.

"Al combate corred bayameses,
Que la patria os contempla orgullosa.
No temais una muerte gloriosa,
Que morir por la patria es vivir.

En cadenas vivir es morir,
En afrenta y oprobio sumidos.
Del clarin escuchad el sonido,
A las armas valientes corred."

When the song finished, Bunnye asked Ricardo to interpret the words of the song in English and he said he would be happy to translate it for her.

"Hasten to battle, men of Bayamo,
For the homeland looks proudly to you.
You do not fear a glorious death,
Because to die for the country is to live.

To live in chains,
Is to live in dishonor and ignominy.
Hear the clarion call,
Hasten brave ones to battle."

"Thank you, Mr. Ricardo," Bunnye said. "I appreciate you interpreting that for me."

"You are quite welcome, sweetheart," he said.

"You know, Mr. Ricardo, folks are a lot more alike than unalike," Bunnye continued, sounding very grown up. "Most everyone loves freedom. Even those folks who claim they don't. If they didn't love it so much, then why would so many people risk their lives each year trying to come to our country?"

"You are so right, Bunnye," he agreed with her. "My folks gave up everything to come here. My mother, however, was able to at least smuggle in her rosary and her gold wedding band. When we came to this country, my father went to work as one who helped clean up a big garage for a man who owned a big trucking company. Later, my father expressed an interest in mechanics. His degree, you know, was in mechanical engineering."

"Oh, I didn't know that," Bunnye said, seeming extremely interested in the conversation.

"Oh, yes," Ricardo continued. "He studied in Germany in the nineteen-fifties, and he was always tinkering with farm machinery, our automobiles, our trucks, even motorcycles. Mr. Vito Casterelli, the gentleman who owned the trucking company, watched my father working and he sent him to diesel mechanic school, which Papi finished in record time. From that point forward, he quickly advanced in the company, saved his money, and my mother, who had never even boiled water in Cuba, worked as a maid at one of the resort hotels on Miami Beach. She saved her money, too."

"Oh, wow," Bunnye said.

"When Mr. Casterelli's health failed, he offered my father the opportunity to purchase the company. He arranged the terms in such a way that my parents, within five years, owned the company. That was the beginning of the Fernandez Trucking Company. It took hard work, Bunnye. It took sacrifice, and it took them appreciating faith, family, and freedom."

"Mama Tee says the same thing," Bunnye told him. "Like I said before, I think folks, no matter where they live or from where they come, are a lot more alike than unalike. I think God must be the color of water, Mr. Ricardo. I think he sees everyone just the same."

Ricardo's mother overheard the conversation and said, "Right you are, my child. Right you are."

The rest of the evening was spent with a lot of laughter and joy, but Dee Dee's Aunt Hattie and Aunt Nanny managed to get everyone out of the house by eleven o'clock. Ricardo gave Dee Dee a long and passionate goodnight kiss at the front door.

"Don't try sneaking back here, Cuban boy," Mama Tee warned him. "Bad luck seeing the bride the day of her marriage."

"I understand, Mama Tee," he said. "I will see my beautiful bride at the altar tomorrow," he added, and then he turned back to Dee Dee. "Goodnight, sweetheart," he said, and he kissed her hand as if he was a prince and she was his princess.

Chapter 27

New Year's Eve dawned sunny and bright with a crisp coolness in the air. Miss Sissy arrived at Hattie's house just after nine o'clock to begin styling everyone's hair, as Madame Hortense and Anna Mary made certain everyone's outfits were turned out to perfection.

The old sanctuary at St. Mary's would only hold about a hundred people, which is why the guest list had to be limited. Some of Ricardo's family, and he had a lot of relatives, were a tad miffed about not being included, but Anna Mary made it plain to them that the guest list was distributed as evenly as possible.

Many of Dee Dee's friends didn't make it into the sanctuary, either, including Reverend and Mrs. Linton, Mark Evers, Miss Sissy's assistant for many years, and Judge and Mrs. Wesson. They were all were invited to the reception following the wedding at Camp EZ, though, and the majority of them accepted, realizing that St. Mary's was indeed a small church.

The old Victorian sanctuary, with its beautiful stained glass windows, had purposely been minimally decorated according to Anna Mary's wishes. On either side of the altar were two large arrangements of white and cream colored roses, as well as huge Asiatic lilies, and Phalaenopsis orchids. Asparagus and fishtail fern had been utilized to give the arrangements a light, airish look; not heavy or cumbersome.

Other than one small arrangement of white roses in the foyer of the church near the guest registry, these were the only adornments for the church. Since the wedding was at two in the afternoon, no candles were necessary.

The elder attendants, Destini, Wanda Faye and Nadine, were resplendent in tea-length dresses of midnight blue velvet. The sashes on the dresses were done in light ecru colored satin. Each dress featured long sleeves and scalloped necklines, and they were full skirted and low-waisted, evoking a look of the nineteen-twenties.

Each of the attendants also wore an ecru colored mantilla, which was a traditional Spanish laced veil, and they carried a small nosegay of cream colored and white roses.

As the organist struck the chords of "The Voice that Breathed O'er Eden", Dee Dee, the lovely and always stunningly beautiful Deborah Delphine Wilson, waltzed down the aisle on the arm of her beloved cousin, Carl Alvin.

The first two who started shedding tears were Ricardo and his brother, Justo, who were standing at the altar, and then Phil Jr. joined in, followed by just about everyone else in the sanctuary.

Dee Dee was a sight to behold, dressed in her great-grandmother Wilson's wedding dress that was designed by the House of Worth in Paris back in the nineteen-twenties. Madame Hortense had done a splendid job, and in quite short order, too, getting it fitted for Dee Dee's perfect hourglass figure. The dress featured the same drop-waisted style as the dresses worn by the attendants. The Jarrellson veil, however, was what made the dress come alive.

Anna Mary was one of the few north Floridians, anywhere, who had a diamond and pearl tiara. It had been worn by her great-grandmother Jarrellson when she was presented at Buckingham Palace in the early nineteen-twenties before King George and Queen Alexandra.

The tiara held the point d'esprit veil in place and trailed behind Dee Dee down the aisle of the church. It was held by the two younger attendants, Mary Selena and Bunnye, who were dressed identically in dresses of ecru colored silk. They wore similar small lace chapel caps and on their hands were ecru colored velvet gloves.

"Don't they look beautiful?" Destini said to Mama Tee, who merely nodded in agreement, as she couldn't actually see.

As the marriage mass continued in Latin, those within the sanctuary, even those who couldn't understand the words, seemed to appreciate the love in the eyes of the bride and the groom.

Dee Dee and Ricardo, indeed, were a beautiful couple. In the eyes of God, family and friends, they knelt at the altar rail together, partook of the blessed sacraments, repeated their vows, and then listened to a song being sung by one of the young parishioners of the church by the name of Alicia Gonzalez. Alicia was home on holiday break from a prominent Catholic college in New York where she was majoring in music. She gave a stunning vocal performance of the song, "Ave Maria".

When the priest finally pronounced Dee Dee and Ricardo man and wife, everyone clapped and cheered, as fresh tears flowed down smiling faces. As the newly wedded couple walked down the aisle toward the front door of the sanctuary, Dee Dee was so happy that she couldn't stop smiling. Of course, there wasn't a dry eye in the house by this time. Even the priest seemed overcome with emotion.

The reception that followed at Camp EZ was, in every way, a north Florida reception, except for the seafood gumbo made by Miss Sissy's handsome young friend, Justin Boudreaux. Everyone raved about his gumbo, even Mama Tee, who said, just like Destini had said back in New Orleans, that it was the first crawfish she had ever eaten.

Justin seemed to be having the time of his life, dancing and celebrating with the wedding guests. Many folks commented to Miss Sissy that she had the most handsome escort at the party. One individual at the party, who seemed most drawn to Justin, was Lady Arabella Keyes, the aunt of young Mary Selena, who had flown over from England just to be at the wedding.

She was at least seven years older than Justin, but it

was evident from the get-go that the titled English lady was more than just a little attracted to the young Creole gentleman from Louisiana.

No one thought much about it, until the band asked Destini to come to the microphone and sing a sultry song for the bride and groom. Just seconds after Ricardo and Dee Dee started dancing to the song, Lady Arabella practically dragged Justin out onto the dance floor. She held him close to her bosom for a long, long time, as the two slow-danced to the music and listened to Destini's version of Norah Jones' "Come Away With Me".

When the two of them finally came off the dance floor, Dee Dee couldn't hold back any longer.

"Honey, are you enjoying yourself?" she asked Lady Arabella.

"Why, yes, I am… very much so," she replied, still holding onto Justin's hand, as if he was her sexual servant.

"I am so glad," Dee Dee said through clenched teeth, obviously quite angry that her special dance with her new husband had just been trampled on. "May I ask you, Lady Arabella, what would you say has been the most enjoyable part of the wedding festivities?"

"Well, that would be hard to say," Lady Arabella said, as she quickly pondered the question. "I suppose I would have to say I was truly, truly impressed with the Louisiana gumbo, as well as the delicious wedding cake, and, of course, the dancing, and Destini's wonderful voice."

"Uh-huh," Dee Dee said, wickedly smiling at her. "Well, I am so pleased you have enjoyed yourself here around the banks of the Suwannee. We aim to please."

Since Dee Dee was preoccupied with her new husband, and rightly so, as well as trying to keep his family entertained, she asked Destini, Wanda Faye, Nadine and Miss Sissy to keep their eyes on Lady Arabella and Justin for the remainder of the night.

"I don't know how much good it'll do," Miss Sissy said. "After all, the man is one heck of a hunk, ain't he? You can't blame her for trying."

"Just the same, try to keep an eye on them," Dee Dee repeated.

A little later, Nadine happened to overhear Lady Arabella ask Justin if he could drive one of the wagons down to the river and back.

"Of course, I can," he told her. "Let me just make a stop in the men's room first, and then your chariot will await you, m' lady," he coddled her.

"Excellent," she said. "I'll grab us a bottle of champagne in the mean time."

About five minutes later, the two of them snuck out the backdoor hand in hand.

"Well, now, I see you put three quilts in the back of that wagon," Nadine said to Wanda Faye, as they stood behind the bushes watching the two lovebirds leave. "Thinking ahead, were you?"

"Just using common sense, honey," Wanda Faye told her, as she stifled a laugh. "I could tell by the way that English gal was eyeing that Louisiana coon ass that there would be more going on during that little wagon ride than just looking at the stars. Trust me. Might as well be in comfort."

"You naughty girl," Nadine said, giggling, as the horse and wagon took off faster than a scared rabbit.

"Hey, the man said he could handle the wagon," Wanda Faye said, laughing out loud now. "How were we to know?"

"Maybe Lady Arabella can get control of that darn horse."

"You mean like she's got control over Justin?" Wanda Faye asked.

"You catch on fast, girl."

One thing that came out during the reception, which really didn't surprise anyone, was when Phil Jr. explained that the investigation into the groundwater contamination had hit a huge roadblock and that it would probably be months, if not years away from being resolved.

"There has been a serious lack of cooperation and loads of red tape that have hampered the investigation," he said. "I promise to stay on top of it, though."

"That's my boy," Destini said, and she hugged him. "I know you'll eventually get to the bottom of it."

Later that evening, the fireworks display over Camp EZ was truly magnificent and it lasted for a good twenty minutes, compliments of Sheriff Bartow Lewis. Destini had asked that a special firework be designed that looked like a heart. Inside of the heart in cursive letters, she wanted "D" and "R" for Dee Dee and Ricardo. The fireworks company didn't disappoint her or Dee Dee and Ricardo.

"Here's to the sweetest, lovingest, most adorable couple in the whole wide world!" Destini announced, as she raised her champagne flute in the air. "May you love and cherish each other until the cows come home!"

"Well, that's a new one," Dee Dee said, chuckling as she and Ricardo clinked their glasses together. "I love you, Ricardo."

"Oh, baby, I love you, too," he told her, as they toasted each other's undying love to one another.

Chapter 28

Most of the guests who had attended the wedding and the reception gathered together at Camp EZ the next day to eat their black-eyed peas, greens and cornbread, the traditional New Year's Day meal for good luck. They also reflected on the happiness of the wedded couple, who had plans to honeymoon in Barbados. They weren't leaving until next week, though, because of a foul-up at the travel agency. Dee Dee, skillful negotiator that she was, got the travel agency to refund their money, but still allow them to go forward with their travel plans.

"Is she good, or what?" Ricardo asked.

"She sho' is," Destini said.

"Hey, now," Dee Dee protested. "We paid that agency over thirty-five hundred dollars for this honeymoon package and it was their screw-up, so we deserved our money back."

"No one is objecting," Destini told her. "Good job, is all I can say… gettin' that trip for free and all."

Meanwhile, there was one person at the luncheon who didn't seem to be eating with her usual gusto, and that was Mama Tee. When Destini asked her what was wrong, she just shrugged her off and said she was simply tired from the previous day's events.

Later that afternoon, Mama Tee's attitude seemed to brighten up some.

"Destini, I'd like you to take me up to Mr. Hamp's cabin in the woods tomorrow," Mama Tee said. "I jus' wanna go and sit in the cabin and talk wid my boy one more time. Can you do that for me, honey?"

"I'm kinda busy tomorrow, Mama Tee," Destini told her.

Mama Tee was persistent, though, so Destini finally, yet reluctantly, agreed to take her to the cabin the next morning at around eight-thirty. Mama Tee was all bundled up and waiting on her porch the next day when Destini and Bunnye pulled up into her yard. The temperature had dropped dramatically overnight and it was still in the low forties, so it was quite chilly.

Once they arrived at the cabin, which only took about ten minutes, Destini built a fire in the fireplace of the front room and Mama Tee settled herself in an antique rocking chair just a few feet away from the warmth of the kindling firewood.

Bunnye wrapped a warm afghan across Mama Tee's shoulders and put another one on her lap, while Destini administered Mama Tee's morning insulin injection. Afterward, Destini placed a cup of hot coffee and a peeled orange that she had brought along with her on a small table next to the rocking chair.

As Mama Tee rocked back and forth, humming an old spiritual to herself, tears began to flow from behind her dark glasses, although, neither Destini nor Bunnye noticed them.

Just then, Destini's cell phone rang and she answered it. It was Nadine reminding her about an appointment with an important client who wanted to rent all of the guest rooms at Camp EZ for a huge fundraiser they were throwing on Valentine's Day.

"The guy's name is Bob Masters and he's supposed to be there at around nine, nine-thirty," Nadine told her.

"Oh, no, I completely forgot," Destini said. "I'm with Mama Tee right now at Mr. Hamp's old place."

"Do you want me to handle it?" Nadine asked. "I might be a little late, though. Maybe too late, now that I think about it. I've got so much going on at the moment."

"No, that's okay," Destini said. "I'll handle it."

After the two girls hung up, Destini turned to Mama Tee.

"I know we just got here, but I'm goin' need to run back up to the camp for a bit and check on some things," Destini told her. "I'll leave Bunnye here with you."

"Naw, y'all go on," Mama Tee said. "A nice fire, warm and cozy, some little snacks here... I'll be jus' fine."

"Ain't no way I'm leavin' you here by yourself, Mama Tee. Bunnye's stayin' and that's that. I'll be back as quick as I can," Destini said, and she hurried out the door.

As soon as the sound of her truck engine disappeared into the ether, Mama Tee called out to

Bunnye.

"Honey, I'd like you to do me a big favor," she said to Bunnye.

"Sure, Mama Tee. Anything," Bunnye told her.

"I'd like you to go back to my place and look in the top drawer of my old sideboard… you know… the one Miss Lillian gave to me from the Brayerford house when Mr. Hamp was born. There's some old letters and pictures there. I'd like for you to look through them with me while I'm sittin' here."

"You want me to go now?" Bunnye asked her.

"If you would, please," Mama Tee said. "There should still be an old bicycle in the back somewhere."

"Are you sure it's okay if I leave you here alone?"

"Aww, now, don't you fret over this old woman. I'll be fine. You just bring me those old letters and pictures, okay?'

"Okay," Bunnye said. "You know, if they're that important, I could scan them for you later today, so that they'll be digitized and safe for eternity."

"Honey, I knows about scammin' and I knows about bammin', but I knows nuttin' 'bout scannin'. If you say it's a good thing, then, honey, you go right ahead."

Bunnye laughed and said, "Yes, ma'am. In fact, I took my computer and my scanner over to Aunt Essie's the other day to scan some documents for Uncle Duke."

"That's wonderful, little girl. Now, you go on and do like I asked. I wants to jus' sit and talk to my boy for a while. You go on, now. I'll be all right."

Mama Tee was humming to herself and gently rocking back and forth when Bunnye left. It took her about twenty minutes for Bunnye to ride back to Mama Tee's place, especially since the road was mostly soft sand and the bike's tires were a little low on air. Once inside, she went straight to the sideboard in Mama Tee's bedroom. It was a beautiful piece of Victorian furniture that bespoke the prominence of Lillian Adamson Brayerford's family.

She opened the drawer and found a large manila envelope that was overflowing with papers and photographs, just where Mama Tee said it would be. One photo that was sticking out of the envelope was of her mother as a little girl holding the hand of a much younger Mama Tee.

Bunnye got curious and dumped out some of the contents. She found a letter from Mrs. Lillian Adamson Brayerford thanking Mama Tee for helping her in the delivery of Hamp Brayerford Jr. It was dated Christmas Day, 1927.

She also found a warranty deed. She didn't know a lot about legal stuff, but in reading the description, she found that while Dee Dee and Carl Alvin owned the acres of land on which Camp EZ was situated, it seemed her grandmother owned all the land leading down to the camp on either side of the road.

"Wow," she said. "I wonder if Mama knows about this."

The last piece of paper she found was a scribbled

note that Mama Tee had evidently recently written because the ink was still smudgy. Since Mama Tee was basically blind, it was a little difficult to decipher her writing. From what she could gather, this is what the note stated:

"If you're reading this letter, it's because I am dying and I plan to go the best way I know how. I don't need no doctor to tell me so. I jus' know it's my time to go. You have to trust me, especially you, my dear, sweet Destini. I refuse to become more of a burden to my family than I already am. I hope you understand. I am leaving this world now. Jus' know that I love you all more than I could ever express.
With all my love and affection,
Lillian Tecola Wilson, your Mama Tee

Bunnye was in shock and she read it again… and again, just to be sure she was reading it correctly. Then, she began to cry. As her tears soaked her face, she thought she smelled smoke. It was strong, too, and seemed very close. When she looked out the window, she saw flames shooting up above the tree line.

"Oh, no!" she screamed. "That fire looks like it's right by my daddy's cabin! Oh, no! Mama Tee!"

She left all the papers and the photos behind and took off on the bike, pedaling as fast as she could. By the time she reached the cabin it was almost fully engulfed in flames. She reached into her pocket, grabbed her cell phone and called her mother.

"Mama!" she screamed. "Mama! It's daddy's cabin!

It's burning up! Mama Tee is inside! She's burning up inside the cabin!"

Destini rushed out onto the porch of Camp EZ and saw the billowing smoke coming from the direction of the cabin.

"Bunnye!" Destini screamed into the phone. "Bunnye, you stay out of dat cabin! You hear me, Bunnye?! It's too late, honey! Stay out of dat cabin! I'm callin' 9-1-1 right now!" she yelled, and she immediately ended the call and then punched in those three fateful numbers.

Bunnye heard what her mother said, but she didn't obey.

"I can't stand here and do nothing!" she wailed. "Mama Tee! Mama Tee! Can you hear me?" she yelled into the cabin from the front porch. "Mama Tee! I'm comin' after you! Don't worry!"

As Destini raced down the road in her pickup, kicking up dust and stones in her wake, she could hear the sirens in the distance and hoped they would make it to the old cabin in time. She was praying the whole way as tears ran down her face. Two times she nearly ran off the road she was so distraught. She had the windows down in the truck and the closer she got, the smokier it became. Two fire trucks were coming up behind her and she pulled over momentarily to let them pass.

The dark waters of the Suwannee River ran swiftly by the burning cabin that day, but not a drop of water from the river's bed could stop the blazing fire from destroying one of the most precious things Destini had ever known. By the time the fire department and the rescue team arrived, there was nothing left of the cabin, other than the foundation and lots of burning embers, as well as about half an acre of blazing timber behind the cabin. It took many hours for the firefighters to find the remnants of what used to be Mama Tee.

Bunnye was lying close to what used to be the front porch with a white sheet over her body. There wasn't a mark on her, she wasn't burned or anything, but she was dead just the same. Repeated attempts to revive her had failed as Destini watched in horror.

Later that day, Destini learned that the firefighters had found two small cans of lighter fluid right near the still smoldering fireplace. The cans were badly charred from the fire, but still identifiable. All Destini knew was that they were two things that were not there when she left Mama Tee and Bunnye in the cabin that morning.

She also learned that night that Bunnye's death wasn't the result of smoke inhalation, but from her heart that gave out as she attempted to enter the burning building. Dr. Campbell's grandson told an hysterical Destini that Bunnye's deep shock at the sight of the blazing fire, combined with a defective heart valve inherited from her father, was most likely what had caused her death.

All Destini could think about for hours afterward, was the dream she kept having about the fallen deer and the vanishing ducks.

Mama Tee's words after Destini told her about the

dream replayed in her head over and over again.

"The part about them deer comin' to the water to drink, and then fallin' over... well, I ain't real sure on that one, but I believe all it means is they's folks in your life who care about you," Mama Tee had told her. "Now, the part about the ducks... two of 'em jus' disappearin' like that? Honey, I'm afraid it's about some people close to you who's gonna die soon. One of 'em is gonna leave this earth with a lil' bit 'o warnin', but the other one will be leavin' suddenly... very suddenly, and it will be a shock to everyone."

"Indeed, it was," Destini thought, as she cried herself to sleep.

Chapter 29

Nadine, Wanda Faye, Dee Dee and Carl Alvin all thought they knew the meaning of grief and pain until they witnessed Destini's total and complete breakdown.

When Dr. Eugene Campbell called Destini and told her that Bunnye's body was ready for her at the funeral home, Destini dropped the phone and turned to her friends, frozen in time for a few seconds.

"I can't go by myself," she finally said. As she stood in the kitchen, her entire body began to tremble out of control. "I can't go by myself!" she cried again.

Everyone there was weeping, including Duke and Essie, and even Miss Sissy, who had cancelled her flight back to New Orleans when she heard about the tragedy. As always, it was Dee Dee who took control of the situation. She asked everyone to follow her and Destini over to the funeral home in Turpricone.

After pulling into the parking lot thirty minutes later, Dee Dee got out of her SUV. Then, she went around and opened the passenger's side door. She drew in her breath, straightened her shoulders, and said, "Come with me, Destini."

She took Destini's hand in hers, and Wanda Faye took her other hand. Essie and Duke followed behind them with Nadine, Miss Sissy and Carl Alvin just a few steps away.

Into the morgue they went and there lay Easter Bunnye Wilson "Brayerford". She looked absolutely beautiful, dressed in a white gown that Essie had brought over earlier. There wasn't one single mark on her face, and her long eyelashes were as beautiful as they ever were.

Destini walked over to her child, bent down and kissed her on the lips and then on the cheeks.

"Oh, my baby. Oh, my sweet, baby girl. What I'm goin' do now? Oh, my baby!" she wailed, and then she started screaming.

The sound of her wailing voice went way beyond grief; it found its origins in the deepest parts of the heart and the soul. Just like unconditional love, it had no pride, no pretension, and no boundaries.

Dee Dee motioned for Dr. Campbell and then whispered something in his ear. Destini then turned to Dee Dee and looked at her like a crazed woman.

"I know what you doing, Dee Dee, and you, too, Dr. Campbell," Destini said, calmly, but firmly, and with a fire in her eyes. "I know you want to give me somethin' to ease my pain, but no, thank you. I got to go through this in my own way."

Then she screamed again, and fell across her child's body. Grief, like love, can either be a comfort or a monster. In this case, everyone knew it was the latter.

As their friend, their kinswoman cried it out over her child, and as Essie held her and Dee Dee held her,

Destini abruptly and completely stopped crying. There was a dark stillness in the room that felt worse than death. It was worse than anyone's wildest imagination could even comprehend. Then, everyone watched in horror as Destini reached into her pocketbook and pulled out a snub-nose .38 revolver. It was a gun that she was licensed to carry and she always kept it in her purse, in case she had to kill a snake, or if she needed it for her own personal protection, is what she always told anyone who asked.

Before anyone could stop her, she opened her mouth, put the barrel inside, and she cocked the trigger. A collective choking gasp from everyone in the room was all that she heard at first.

Soon, the voice that connected with her was not the voice of any of the usual suspects, like Dee Dee or Nadine, who were now yelling at her to drop the gun. Indeed, everyone was more than a bit stunned when they watched Miss Sissy go right up to Destini's face and speak, as she stared at the butt end of the gun. Right behind her was Sheriff Bartow Lewis.

"Destini, honey, give the gun to me," Miss Sissy softly said, as she held out her hand. "Give it to me," she said a bit louder. "Give that damned gun to me and stop this bullshit!" she finally yelled, staring straight into Destini's eyes.

Everyone in the room seemed to be suspended in time and it was eerily quiet all of a sudden. Destini's eyes scanned the room and she saw all the frightened faces looking back at her. Then, as an innocent child would hand a friend a piece of candy to be shared, Destini did as Miss Sissy asked. She gently removed the gun from her mouth and handed it over to her.

"Now, I'm gonna tell you something, girl," Miss Sissy said. "There was more than one reason I came to Campbell County. This is something nobody knows except this man right here," she said, grabbing onto the sheriff's arm. "I had a little girl, Audrey Blair Paquette. Her daddy was the man who owned the cotton gin where my daddy worked for years. He sent me to beauty school to help me and because he knew I was pregnant. When I had that baby, God, she was the world to me. One day, when we were in downtown New Orleans, she somehow pulled away from me and in an instant she was hit by a car and killed. I thought I'd die. I wanted to die. Trust me, I wanted to, but Destini, honey, God didn't take you home. You're still here, baby. He took Mama Tee and he took your baby and that's awful. That's truly, truly awful, but he didn't take you. There's a reason you are alive right now, and I'm thinking you need to give God a chance. Give him a chance, honey. The road will be rough and full of stones, but give God a chance."

Destini's expression changed and she looked directly at the sheriff.

"Thank y'all for coming, Sheriff," she said. "I sho' do appreciate it. You one of the finest men and one of the best men I ever knew, but you're a fool. A fool... and all these years I wanted to say that to you."

"Now, Destini, I know you're grieving, honey, but

I'm on your side," he said.

"I knows dat, and I'm on yours. I loves you," she said and she went up to him and kissed him on the cheek. "Grief is dis room. It's here. Oh, Lord, it's on me!" she screamed.

She screamed so piercingly loud that Carl Alvin, who was standing right behind her, had to cover his ears. Then, she calmed down a bit.

"Sheriff, love is standing right beside you and you have closed your damn fool eyes to it for thirty years. Out of what? Pride?" Destini asked him, although, she wasn't expecting him to respond. "Hey, ain't no pride here. They's no pride in love and they's no pride in grief. None... absolutely none, whatsoever."

With that, Destini turned and walked out of the room. Miss Sissy looked at the sheriff and just shrugged her shoulders.

"Don't ask me," she said, and then she smiled at him.

Chapter 30

The parishioners of Mt. Nebo AME Church had abandoned all pretenses for any of their guests on this mournful day. They were obviously appreciative they were present, but this service was not about them. It was about Lillian Tecola Wilson; icon, matriarch, and a legend known as Mama Tee to her loved ones and good friends. It was also about her great-great granddaughter, twelve-year-old Easter Bunnye Wilson (Brayerford), whose life was cut way too short.

Two ivory white caskets with sterling silver handles and adornments were sitting in front of the altar inside the sanctuary. One casket was opened with a cascading spray of pink and white roses. The other one was closed and covered with an exquisite full casket spray of the same pink and white roses.

Bunnye was wearing the ecru colored silk dress she had worn in Dee Dee's wedding, and her hair was styled in a beautiful French braid.

Family members from across the nation had made extreme sacrifices in order to come home for the funeral. One cousin in Seattle, Alisha Jones, had cashed her entire month's check just to buy two roundtrip plane tickets for her and her husband, which left their rent unpaid. She said she didn't care, though, because there was no way she would miss coming home to pay her respects to Mama Tee and Bunnye.

Another cousin rode a Greyhound bus for ten hours after pawning his guitar and trumpet for the ticket. He said he didn't know how he was going to get back home, unless he hitchhiked. Yet another cousin in New York sold her wedding rings to pay for plane fare.

In a standing room only sanctuary, the large, white robed choir softly began singing, "Nearer My God To Thee". Then, Reverend Aloysius Jackson began the age old litany, "I am the resurrection and the life, sayeth the Lord."

Augustine Jackson, the reverend's brother and owner of the local African American funeral home, stood beside the two caskets, as the procession of family members took one last look at Bunnye and gently touched the casket holding what was left of Mama Tee's remains.

Alisha, the cousin from Seattle, was heavily veiled and beautifully attired in a black suit. As she approached Mama Tee's casket, she screamed without shame or abandon, "Mama Tee!" Her husband had to catch her when she nearly fainted seconds later.

What few expected, however, was Dee Dee's reaction when she, her husband Ricardo, and Carl Alvin approached the two caskets. Mama Tee had been a haven for both Dee Dee and Carl Alvin since they were babies, and her death hit both of them hard.

Dee Dee had watched Bunnye grow up right before her eyes. She was a beautiful young girl, who was about to become a teenager with dreams as big as the sky before being abruptly called up into heaven.

In Dee Dee's arms she carried two bouquets of the deepest, darkest, long-stemmed American Beauty red roses God had ever created. Destini and Essie were sitting side by side on the first pew with Duke on the other side of Essie. When Dee Dee approached them, she turned to Sister Viola Jackson, who was standing at the end of the pew. Viola lifted Dee Dee's veil for her. Then, Dee Dee bent down and kissed Destini on the cheek before handing her one of the rose bouquets. She presented the other bouquet to Essie.

A moment later, Dee Dee motioned for Carl Alvin and Ricardo to go to their seats and sit with the family. Then, she did something that no one in Campbell County had ever witnessed before. She bent down again and stayed on her knees at Destini's feet, handkerchief in hand, and there she remained until the service was over.

She had rendered the most humble service of love and respect, which had Destini in tears. The congregation took it all in and seemed to instinctively know that Dee Dee was humbling herself not only before her friend, but before God himself to offer the greatest comfort she could.

Minutes later, after everyone had paid their respects, the elderly minister mounted the pulpit. He held up his hand and motioned for everyone to be seated.

"Two days before Mama Tee left this earth, she

and I had a conversation," Reverend Jackson began. "She said to me, "Preacher, I am ready to go home. I am ready to go home. I have seen my name on that roll up in heaven, and I am ready to go home." Keeping that in mind, her granddaughter, Destini Wilson, is going to come and sing."

Dee Dee looked up at Destini, who seemed to have composed herself quite well, and asked, "Honey, are you sure?"

Destini nodded, and said, "I'm sure."

Dee Dee helped her up onto the platform and then sat back down on the front pew next to Essie. As Destini began to sing, Dee Dee broke down in her own tears of anguish.

> *"Steal away, steal away,*
> *Steal away to Jesus,*
> *Steal away, steal away, home.*
> *I ain't got long to stay here."*

When she finished, everyone was in tears All that could be heard throughout the sanctuary was weeping and sniffling, and folks blowing their noses, as the congregation fought to control their heartache at the loss of two beautiful people.

After the church service, the remainder of the day was taken up with the burials of both Bunnye and Mama Tee. They were laid to rest on a high bluff overlooking the Suwannee River in an ancient burial ground where scores of African Americans from

Campbell County had been buried.

In the middle of the burial ground, Destini had ordered the erection of a monument. It was an angel made out of carved stone with her wings outspread, and in the angel's hand was a broken chain. The inscription at the bottom read:

> *To the scores of good men and women buried here,*
> *Who worked and toiled, and who, for many years,*
> *Only had the earth as their memorial.*
> *In loving memory.*
> *Free at last."*

The inscription referred to the countless number of slaves who were buried in the cemetery that had once belonged to the Jarrellson family, the Adamson family, the Campbell's and the Brayerfords.

When the monument was placed there two days ago, Destini felt that now their spirits could speak through the angel to her and the hundreds of others who would come to visit their loved ones. There was now an outward acknowledgement that the lives they lived on this earth counted for something.

Phil Jr. had earlier asked if he could make a short speech about Mama Tee and Bunnye. Everyone listened attentively to all his kind words as he reminisced.

"There is one thing I must say," he included at the end of his speech. "Miss Destini was the love that held this family together through thick and thin. She is a remarkable woman and one whom I will cherish always," he added, as his eyes welled with tears.

What prompted her to do so, other than maybe she needed absolution for her past sins, was beyond Destini's comprehension, but Anna Mary, with Stanley by her side, made an impromptu speech about how Destini had helped her son Watson. It was very revealing and told the entire story of Watson's unfortunate life in about two minutes flat, warts and all.

"I just want you to know that Stanley and I, and Mary Selena, love you with all our hearts and we share in your grief, Destini. If there is anything we can do for you, please, please, just let us know."

As the hundreds of mourners stood at the gravesite, a long, sleek, black limousine pulled up to the cemetery gate. Moments later, someone completely unexpected emerged from the limousine. It was none other than the most famous African American woman in the nation, as well as one of the wealthiest, Margot Smith.

Margot walked over to the gravesite and she kissed the feet of the angel. Then, she went over to where Destini stood and she whispered something in her ear. Destini nodded her head. Margot then walked up to Reverend Jackson and quietly spoke to him. He, too, nodded his head, and then he stepped back. Then, she removed her sunglasses and handed them to Wanda Faye, who was off to her left.

"Several years ago, this lady asked if I would allow a center for abused women to be named in my honor,"

Margot began, as she motioned toward Wanda Faye.
"It was I, however, who was honored. During that visit
here for the dedication, Mama Tee asked me if I would
allow her to touch my face. When I knelt before her,
and she ran those healing hands over my face, I felt as
if I was in the presence of something truly holy… and I
was. You know what she told me that day? She told me
that I gave her hope," Margot said, as she began to
choke up. "My God, I was the one who was given
hope. I stayed in touch with her since that time, and
each time I spoke with her, she would ask me, "How is
my girl?" Ohh, my heart would just sing."

After many amen's and hallelujah's, and more
weeping from the crowd, Margot continued.

"Today, I am here and we lay to rest the earthly
remains of not only Mama Tee, but also precious little
Bunnye. I can still see her in her little flowered sundress
on the day my car arrived. I had the window down to
breathe in the spring air, and I heard that voice as she
shouted down the drive, "She here, Mama, she here!"

This time, Wanda Faye led the group in more
amen's.

"I know in my own mind that up in Glory, Mr.
Hamp Brayerford, Bunnye's dear departed father, along
with Mama Tee's beloved husband, and several of her
children who have already gone to be with the Lord,
are shouting, "They're here! Mama Tee and Bunnye are
here!"

Destini was doing her best to keep her wits about
her and keep herself standing upright, but it was clear

from the faint smile on her face that she was beginning the healing process.

"There's something else I want to tell you," Margot continued. "I will tell you unashamedly that I am a Christian. I established a ministry a while back, and in light of what happened here recently, I decided to name it in honor of Bunnye and Mama Tee. This ministry reaches out to children here and in Central and South America, as well as in South Africa. I have visited the school I established in South Africa many times already."

"God bless you, Margot," Wanda Faye said.

"After today, many of you may not see Destini for some time," Margot went on. "I talked with her yesterday, and as soon as everyone eats and socializes today, she will be flying with me to South Africa."

There was a collective gasp from the crowd, and then some hushed chatter, as folks tried to absorb the news.

"We will be there for about three months, as I am adding a culinary department to my school," Margot said. "I can't think of a soul more able to teach the girls there how to cook than Destini," she added.

There were a few people in the crowd who looked surprised, but not Dee Dee.

"Good for you, honey," Dee Dee said, and she winked at Destini.

"One more thing," Margot told the crowd. "It just so happens that the National Conference of the AME Church will be held in a neighboring town very close to where Destini and I will be, so she will get to hear all that good gospel singing that she dreamed about after Mr. Hamp passed away. I know it was one of her bucket list dreams and I am so happy that I get to be a part of it, too."

Later that afternoon, Destini said goodbye to everyone and went back to Camp EZ with Dee Dee. Then, she texted, called and even wrote a few notes to certain special friends in between packing for the trip.

Right before she left with Margot, she and Dee Dee shared an emotional farewell hug.

"Don't you worry, Dee Dee," Destini said. "I'll be back."

"I know you will," Dee Dee said. "Camp EZ could use a little respite for a while. It needs time to heal, too, you know. Anyway, you just stay safe, okay?"

"You can count on it," Destini said, and she and Margot took off in the big, black limo, leaving a trail of dust in their wake.

Chapter 31

After about two months into her gig in South Africa, Destini's letters to the girls, Nadine, Wanda Faye and Dee Dee, were mainly about a young man she had met, who was working there in the ministry. He was about ten years younger than her and she referred to him as Reverend Matthew Abamu.

When the three months were about up, she wrote and told the girls she was coming home. She also told them that Matt, which is what she was now calling him, would be coming home with her.

The girls, as well as Carl Alvin, were all abuzz as they waited at Camp EZ for Destini and Matt to arrive. Not surprisingly, a large, black limousine transported them from the airport to the camp. When Destini stepped out, her face was beaming. When Matt emerged it was all over for the girls.

"Oh, my," Nadine whispered to Dee Dee, as they stood on the front porch. "He is quite the handsome man, isn't he?"

"He seems very humble, too," Dee Dee said.

"And friendly looking," Wanda Faye piped up, as she watched him put his arm around Destini.

"Women," Carl Alvin mumbled, shaking his head.

Dee Dee invited them inside and offered a round

of champagne in honor of Destini's return. There was also a large buffet of some of Destini's favorite foods waiting for them in the dining room.

Before they sat down to eat, however, Matt held up his hand, and said, "I have an announcement to make."

"Oh, cool!" Dee Dee squealed. "I hope it's something good!"

"Yes, I believe it is," Matt said, as Destini stood beside him, blushing. "Anyway, I am proud to make this momentous announcement. Two days ago, this beautiful lady became my wife."

After a brief moment of silence and total shock on everyone's faces, pandemonium struck, as Dee Dee, Wanda Faye and Nadine, and even Carl Alvin, began screaming with joy and taking turns hugging the two newlyweds.

"Can y'all believe it?!" Destini cackled. "I'm an old married lady! Oh... I got one more thing to tell y'all. Now, hold your breaths, okay? I'm goin' have a baby! I'm goin' have me another baby! Isn't that amazing? An ol' woman like me! I found out earlier this morning when I stopped by to see Dr. Campbell. Oh... and it's a girl!"

The news about the marriage was exciting enough, but the news about the baby was almost more than everyone could handle, as more pandemonium ensued.

"Oh, honey, that is such wonderful, wonderful news," Dee Dee said, once everyone calmed down. "What will you name her?"

"I'm gonna name her after me, sort of, because this

part of the world and our story is definitely and has always been our destiny. So, yes, her name will be Destiny… with a "Y". What do you think about that?"

"I say thank God for Destiny!" Dee Dee shouted.

"Yes, indeed," Destini said, smiling wide and proud. "Only God could have gifted me with the hope of this destiny," she added, and she kissed her husband square on the mouth.

"Destini, honey, you forgot to mention one more thing," Matt said.

"Huh?" she asked.

"You know… the honeymoon," he whispered to her.

"Oh! Oh, yeah! You'll never guess where me and Matt are going for our honeymoon… our delayed honeymoon, that is, since we ain't had one yet."

"Where?" Wanda Faye asked.

"Yeah, where?" Nadine wanted to know. "Hawaii? The South Pacific?

"Nope," Destini said, shaking her head. "Remember I said I always wanted to go to Washington D.C.? Well, that's where we're going next week. I'll finally be able to see where my baby Phil Jr. works."

"After we visit Niagara Falls, that is," Matt interrupted.

"Oh, honey, that is so exciting," Dee Dee said, and she hugged her. "I'm sure you two will enjoy every minute of it."

Destini Wilson Abamu then looked at her friends,

and at her new husband, and she thought about a quote Mr. Hamp had treasured for many years. It was a quote about the Suwannee River, but she thought it truly applied to her at this moment in time, and it reflected the feelings in her heart. She shared it with her friends and Matt.

"The real Suwannee River does not rise in any part of Georgia. It rises in the highest mountains of the human soul and is fed by the deepest springs in the human heart. It does not empty into any material sea, but into the glorious ocean of unfulfilled dreams."

"A man from New York by the name of James Craig wrote that about Stephen Foster in the old New York Telegram and Evening Mail," Destini explained. "Why is this so, you ask? Because Stephen Foster made the Suwannee River immortal with a song."

Destini knew in her heart, as she looked into the eyes of her friends, that each one of them would one day leave her, or perhaps she would go first, but the one thing she knew for certain was that their destiny would always be the unbreakable chain of love. Yes, unconditional love.

About the Author

White Springs native Johnny Bullard was born in a place where two cities and two counties interconnect on the banks of the historic Suwannee River. His family roots run about seven generations deep into the sandy soil of north central Florida, a place he dearly loves and where his entire life has been spent as an educator, public servant, musical performer and writer.

Born into a family of prolific storytellers, Bullard absorbed all the tales that were told aloud, as well as the ones whispered quietly inside screened porches and around the dining room table when family and close friends gathered together.

Bullard's grasp of the culture and life of this region is expressed by one who has not only lived it, but who loves it and is a part of it. He offers a humorous, poignant and honest voice of a South that is still colorful, vibrant, rich and real. Bullard is as much a part of the region as the historic Suwannee River, immortalized by Stephen C. Foster in the unforgettable tune, "Old Folks at Home".

An old turpentine distillery at the Eight Mile Still on the Woodpecker Route north of White Springs is where Bullard calls home. He boasts four college degrees from Valdosta State University in Georgia, including a B.A. in English. He also did post graduate work at Florida State University in Tallahassee, Florida, and was privileged to be selected to attend the prestigious Harvard Principal's Center at Harvard University in Cambridge, Massachusetts in 1993.

Bullard writes a weekly column, "Around the Banks of the Suwannee", which is published in the *Jasper News* and *Suwannee Democrat* newspapers. He has also written magazine articles for several well known publications including *Forum*, a quarterly publication of the Florida Humanities Council.

His weekly newspaper column always ends with his signature message to all his readers, friends and relatives throughout the region. He writes, "From the Eight Mile Still on the Woodpecker Route north of White Springs, I wish you all a day filled with joy, peace, and above all, lots of love and laughter."

Johnny Bullard

Reviews

I was drawn to the descriptive beauty of Bullard's North Florida, contrasted by the lives of the characters and their story of struggle and triumph. *Laura R.*

The characters are believable and true to life. By story's end, you'll find yourself wanting to move to Seraph Springs to meet Wanda Faye, Nadine and Destini. *Lesleigh*

Truly Southern! A very good read, and written by a talented and eloquent writer. *Dianne Banks*

Old school Southern writing; a fantastic take set in the Deep South by a talented writer. *Charles B. Pennington*

The mystery, intrigue, redemption and "dirty deeds" are spot on; kept me wanting more. *Monica Chambers*

I loved this book! It was like reading about old friends. *Sharron Handley*

This book will keep you turning the pages as you anxiously await what will happen next! *Cathy F.*

Written by a true southern gentleman, Johnny just makes the characters come to life. *Amazon reader*

Mr. Bullard brings to life the true meaning of friends and family, and sharing in ones lives. Johnny is an inspiring writer that can relate to people and their feelings. *Debra Mahaffey*

Secrets is a "can't-put-it-down" kind of book. It grabbed me from the first sentence and held on until the end, especially since I had already read *Nightshade*. Simply a must read for all those who enjoy sharing their secrets with best friends! *Shirley Smith*

Good story with familiar surroundings from growing up in the area. Lots of diversions, too. Another great job by Johnny Bullard. He is a great storyteller. *Amazon reader*

The first book I could not put down, so I'm waiting until I have a rainy day to read *Secrets*. Love the author! *Angela Townsend*

I enjoyed this book very much. I can relate to the small town setting and all of the drama that goes on daily. *Amazon reader*

This book cleared up the mysteries that left you hanging from the first book. I enjoyed both books very much. *Julie D.*

Made in the USA
Columbia, SC
11 October 2017